Jenny Carver—She's a single mom who's working *and* going to law school. Life isn't easy, but she's getting by. Spending a month at a cabin in Maine should be a dream vacation. Except her son hates it—and Ben Sullivan, her very sexy neighbor, is threatening to upset her best-laid plans.

Chris Carver—He didn't want to come to Maine. The cabin's a "dump" and there's no TV. But at least Ben, the guy who lives down the road, is cool—he knows all about canoeing and fly-fishing. If Chris had his way, his mom would marry Ben, not the stuffy lawyer she's engaged to.

Ben Sullivan—The fast lane's not for him. Nothing could make him go back to big-city life or big-city law—not even Jenny....

Dear Reader,

How often do we say, "She's trying to do it all"? Sometimes it's an observation made about a friend or relative. Sometimes we apply it to ourselves. Today's world demands a great deal from us. Jobs are juggled with families, career advancement with home life. Single custodial parents abound, and more often than not that parent is a woman. Almost inevitably, the one caught in the middle of such a situation is a child.

I thought about this when I began to write a story set in the Maine woods. An ideal setting, at first glance, for a mother and child escaping the city for a vacation. But troubles have a way of following no matter where we go, packed into our emotional luggage like toothbrushes in a suitcase.

Jenny, the mother in *Sullivan's Law,* has hopes and dreams for twelve-year-old Chris, and like many other working moms, she's determined to be strong and handle everything herself. Along the way, however, she learns that kids have a way of choosing their own paths, and that seemingly sensible plans can collapse like a house of cards.

The truth is that nobody can do it all. Everyone needs help and love, just as surely as kids need kisses. And sometimes the best-laid plans have to be scuttled. Things we thought were important may have to be forgotten so we can concentrate on love. How to achieve a balance, how to find what works, is the challenge. You can't do it all, perhaps, but there's no reason you can't have it all.

Sincerely,

Amanda Clark

SULLIVAN'S LAW
Amanda Clark

Harlequin Books

TORONTO • NEW YORK • LONDON
AMSTERDAM • PARIS • SYDNEY • HAMBURG
STOCKHOLM • ATHENS • TOKYO • MILAN
MADRID • WARSAW • BUDAPEST • AUCKLAND

ISBN 0-373-03333-8

SULLIVAN'S LAW

This edition published by arrangement with Harlequin Enterprises B. V.

® and TM are trademarks of the publisher. Trademarks indicated with
® are registered in the United States Patent and Trademark Office, the
Canadian Trade Marks Office and in other countries.

Printed in U.S.A.

CHAPTER ONE

JENNY COULD FEEL the first distant throbbing of a headache that she knew would shortly be full-blown. She closed her eyes against it for a moment, then opened them again for another look around the house.

"Is *this* it?" Chris's voice dripped with twelve-year-old scorn. "Boy, what a dump."

Not answering, Jenny walked through the kitchen with its empty, open-doored refrigerator and rusted range into the main room. Through winter-grimed windows the sweep of the lake could be seen, gray and sullen on this overcast day in late June. Inside, the furniture was covered with sheets. The big stone fireplace had a piece of plywood wedged against its opening. She moved to peer into the two bedrooms, one on each side of the main room. Beds with bare mattresses, bureau drawers taken out and replaced upside down.

"What'd they do that for?" Chris was staring at the drawers.

"So mice couldn't get into them." Jenny heard her own voice, weak and distant.

"Jeez." The boy's scorn intensified a notch. "This place is some mess."

Jenny tried to rally and sound cheerful. "Well, it won't take any time to straighten it up. I'll call Mr. and

Mrs. Preston to find out what happened. Maybe they can come right over and give us a hand."

She hurried to the telephone, but there was no dial tone when she picked it up. "Oh. Disconnected, of course. Well, we'll have that fixed tomorrow." She glanced nervously at her son, who was standing just inside the room. Too tall, too thin, too bitter for twelve. She had been counting on this vacation to bring the two of them together, to erase that streetwise expression from his young face. "Anyway, it won't be hard to fix things up for tonight. We'll be okay."

"Yeah?" His hand came out to flick the light switch. Nothing happened.

"Oh, dear." Jenny felt the throbbing in her head increase. A wave of hot anger swept over her as she remembered the telephone conversation with her father a few days before.

"Would you mind our using the house at the lake? Only if you're not planning to go there yourself, of course," she'd said, making an effort to be especially polite. There was a hesitation at the other end of the line, and she could picture her father, hawk-nosed and imperiously handsome, graying hair swept back elegantly. "I just feel ... it might do Chris some good," she rambled on.

He'd ignored the mention of Chris, as he'd ignored the boy's existence for twelve years. "No, Grace and I weren't planning to go to Maine until the first of August," he said at last. "I suppose you could use it if you don't mind being up there by yourself." Again, ignoring Chris.

"I appreciate it," Jenny said, wanting to add "Dad," but finding it awkward. "It's the first real vacation I've had from my job. I hope you don't mind."

"I'll telephone the Prestons to see about having the place opened up," he said stiffly.

"Wonderful. We should be there in a few days." Jenny hesitated. "How's Grace?"

"Very well, thank you."

"Please remember me to her."

He'd hung up without saying goodbye.

"I can't imagine why the Prestons haven't been here to get it ready for us," she said now. She tried to square her shoulders. It seemed a major effort. "But we should be able to manage until tomorrow. Have to rough it a little, that's all."

"Why'd we have to come up here, anyway?" Chris demanded angrily, turning and stamping out of the house.

"Chris, wait . . ." Jenny called after him, but he was gone. She moved to the window and saw him walking down the slope toward the lake. He began picking up stones from the beach and hurling them into the water. Not lazily, as most boys would have, but furiously.

Jenny took a deep breath, trying to hold off utter despair. Crying wouldn't help, either, she reminded herself sternly as she began taking the sheets off the furniture. But her thoughts were gloomy. Hadn't she enough troubles already? Did she really need to have one more thing go wrong?

After she'd uncovered the furniture she took the broom from behind the kitchen door, where it had always been kept. Odd, she thought, that she'd remember such a thing after twelve years. Actually nothing much had changed about the place. Her father's second wife, Grace, hadn't made the alterations Jenny had somehow expected. The house still had its slightly down-at-the-heels look. No gloss, no obvious renovations. One small thing to be grateful for, Jenny thought.

She started sweeping, but made a mental note that the kitchen would need scrubbing tomorrow. Tonight they'd have to find a place to eat out. She'd planned to shop for food and cook dinner here, but there was probably no propane gas in the tank for cooking. An awful thought struck her. She went to the chipped white enamel sink and twisted the faucet. No water. The pipes had been drained for the winter.

Helpless with anger and frustration, she went again to the window and looked at her son, still heaving stones into the lake. Then she wheeled around and pushed out the kitchen door, shouting his name.

"Chris, could you come here and give me a hand, please?" It was an irritated voice, full of impatience. This was exactly the sort of thing she'd resolved *not* to do here. This was supposed to be a vacation where they both learned to talk to each other and to listen. No city distractions, no pressure from work or school. But her voice had sounded just as it had back in Boston—hard-edged and authoritative.

Scowling, her son started up the slope toward the house, walking with maddening slowness. At the same moment a pickup truck appeared around the curve of the wooded drive and pulled up directly in front of her. A man got out, hooked his thumbs in his jeans and looked around, taking in the small car, the house and then her.

"Hi," he said. He looked to be thirty-five or so, with a shock of thick black hair, black eyebrows and a slightly cleft chin. He was tall, broad-shouldered and muscular. Two dogs had gotten out of the truck with him. One was black and appeared to be mostly Labrador retriever. The other was a mixture that defied immediate analysis, a heavy-chested brindle animal with a white streak down its nose.

"Well, finally!" Jenny said as relief washed over her. "I thought no one was going to show up. Could you possibly get in touch with the Prestons for me?"

He regarded her directly. His eyes were dark blue, the lashes long.

"I'm Ben Sullivan," he said. "Apparently you have problems."

"You might say that." Jenny struggled for a light tone, not wanting to show the very real despair she was feeling. "We just got here, and I know we were expected, but...what's happened to the Prestons? They've taken care of this place for years, and my father said he'd ask them to open up the house, but nothing's been done, not a thing, and I don't know what we'll—" She stopped, aware that he had turned and spotted Chris standing a short distance away.

"Hi there," he said.

"Hi." Chris was still wearing the sullen look Jenny hated. The black dog ambled over to him and nuzzled her nose into his hand. Startled, Chris drew his hand away.

"She's harmless," Ben Sullivan said. The other dog hung back behind him, looking wary and tense.

"I'm sorry," Jenny said. "I should have introduced myself. I'm Jenny Carver, and that's my son Chris. You see, the phone isn't connected and the place is a mess and I just don't know what I can—"

"How do you do." The blue-black eyes returned to her and Jenny could see amusement there. She drew herself up a little straighter.

"Well, where *are* the Prestons?" she asked.

"Montana."

"Montana!"

"For a month or so. Daughter's wedding. And a brief Western trip. So if your father tried to call them, he didn't get an answer. Not too many answering machines around Tucker's Pond."

And naturally her father hadn't troubled himself to let her know. Maybe hadn't even bothered to keep track of her address, which probably didn't worry him at all, she thought bitterly.

"You're Buzz Carmichael's daughter?" he asked, his eyes moving over her, sizing her up.

"Yes."

"I see some similarity."

"What do you mean by that?" she demanded.

"Well, Mr. Carmichael likes things done on time, too."

Jenny felt some dignity was in order. "I hate to trouble you, Mr. Sullivan, but if you could possibly help me with one or two things..."

"Sure. I'm filling in for Jack Preston, getting some of the summer places around the lake opened for the season. I was leaving this one until later, because Jack had it marked down for August first." He was still standing by his truck, looking around casually.

Jenny asked, "How'd you know we were here?"

"Stopped at the gas station in town. They told me."

She'd bought gas there. She'd forgotten how efficiently news was disseminated in this part of the world.

She said, "Well, I'm afraid it's going to be a lot of work. There's no water, no lights, no telephone, no way to cook." To her dismay, she heard a quaver in her voice and felt tears threatening.

Ben Sullivan's black eyebrows went up. "Oh, come on. It's not that bad." He seemed to regard the whole matter as something of very little importance. In spite of her frustration, Jenny found herself staring at the tiny cleft in his chin. He made a gesture with one hand. "You've got a whole lakeful of water, for one thing, and I've brought you some for drinking." He reached into the truck and brought out two gallon jugs. "I'll put up some screens for you and take the cap off the chimney, if that'll help."

Jenny took the two plastic jugs from him. "Thank you," she said. "But there isn't any... We can't..." She trailed off helplessly.

"It's just lake water that's piped in, anyway," he said. "And you'll have the bottled water to drink. The lake's clean enough for any other uses."

He tossed a plastic bucket to Chris, who hadn't moved. The boy missed it and leaned over to retrieve it. "How about bringing up some water, Chris?" he suggested.

The boy threw him a resentful glance and made his way down to the dock. The black dog trotted after him. As Ben Sullivan went out to the shed behind the house and brought back screens, the other dog stuck close to him, but it refused to come inside with him. Jenny was happy about that. The way the dog stared at her frightened her a little.

"You might want a fire tonight. Once the sun goes down it's apt to be chilly. I take it you won't be opening up the guest house."

"No, I won't need it," Jenny answered, watching him warily, feeling what she recognized in herself as typical big-city caution around a stranger. Actually she hadn't even explored the little guest house yet. It was the only change she'd noticed since her arrival. She could see the place through the trees about fifty yards away from the main house and knew it had been built since her father married Grace. It blended with the older structure, however, and was quite unobtrusive. She supposed Grace and her father needed it for their frequent entertaining.

"I'm running behind in my own work today, but I'll see about getting the power back on for you tomorrow," Ben Sullivan went on. "Then we can get the pump and boiler going so you'll have hot water. After that we'll have some propane delivered and hook up the telephone, and everything will be back to normal."

Chris returned, still scowling, the bucket banging against his side and the water slopping onto his jeans. He put it on the kitchen floor and bolted back out the door at once. Ben Sullivan watched him go but said nothing.

"There. You can use that for washing up." He yanked open the big hinged windows, which resembled French doors, hung the screens and let the windows stand open to let in the fresh pine-scented air. Jenny took a deep breath, feeling a little better in spite of everything.

There was a sudden sound of splashing, and she ran to the window to look anxiously down at the dock. The black dog was swimming vigorously, a stick in her mouth. While Jenny watched, the dog returned to shore, dropped the stick at Chris's feet and shook herself vigorously. Jenny saw Chris shrink back, but after a moment he picked up the stick and tossed it into the water again. The dog leapt after it.

"Rocket likes to play." Ben Sullivan's voice was so near that Jenny started. When she turned she could see the muscles in his broad chest and arms under his plaid shirt. He was regarding her in that half-amused way, and she felt herself coloring again. She took a quick backward step. "I'll see about the cap on that chimney now," he said.

Jenny, feeling confused but slightly less helpless, went about setting up the two bedrooms, locating clean sheets and making beds, turning the dresser drawers right side up. From outside she could hear the man humming and now and then whistling. She peeked out the window and watched him go to the shed and return with a ladder. He put it against the side of the house and began climbing the rungs. She could hear his footsteps on the roof. When she returned to the main room, he was back and had already pulled away the plywood that covered the stone fireplace opening. He was kneeling on the hearth, his back to her, brushing dirt into a dustpan. For a moment she stood still, watching.

"Now you can light that fire tonight if you need it."

Jenny was surprised. How had he known she was there?

"Thank you," she managed. "Except I'm afraid there isn't any firewood."

"Oh, we can take care of that," he said easily. He got to his feet and went out, carrying the dustpan. Jenny followed him to the doorway, watched him dump the dirt and glance at Chris, standing with his shoulders slumped and gazing moodily out over the water. The sun had come out from behind the clouds. The black dog had given up swimming and was lying on the dock.

"Hey, Chris!" the man called.

The boy didn't turn, and Jenny said, "I think he's got his Walkman on." She wished Ben Sullivan wouldn't try to involve Chris. The man was altogether too big, too domineering. It would be impossible for Chris to relate to someone like that. But before she could say anything more, Ben was heading down toward the lake. Jenny saw him get Chris's attention, talk to him briefly, and then the two of them started back up the slope, Chris trailing clumsily behind, the black dog following. Chris was still wearing his Walkman and his expression was decidedly cross.

Ben whistled for the two dogs. "Come on, Rocket." The friendly black one, still damp, ambled up to the truck and jumped in. "You too, Blaze," Ben ordered, and the powerful-looking dog, who had been crouching in the brush, followed.

"Chris can give me a hand," Ben said to Jenny. "We'll be right back." He swung up into the driver's side, and Chris, without looking at his mother, got into the passenger side. It took him two tries to make the high step, and to Jenny he suddenly looked so young and vulnerable her heart went out to him.

The truck roared off down the narrow dirt drive. All at once Jenny was seized with anxiety. She shouldn't let Chris go off with a strange man. She knew nothing about this Ben Sullivan. And he had that awful drill-sergeant way about him. Was he to be trusted? You heard such dreadful stories. She went inside to start unpacking, but came back to the door every few minutes to look out nervously. No phone, so she couldn't even call the police if she needed them, and who knew how far this man and her son had gone or where....

When the truck rounded the curve again she let her breath out in a sob and hurried back inside so they wouldn't know she'd been watching. She heard the thunk-thunk of wood being stacked. Hurriedly she changed out of her city clothes, slipping into jeans and a green sweatshirt that said Celtics across the front. She put on running shoes and ran a brush through her shoulder-length brown hair. Briefly she glanced in the mirror over the bureau. Amber eyes looked back at her as she applied a light touch of lipstick.

When he saw her at the back door, Ben Sullivan looked her over with a kind of lazy approval but said nothing. He and Chris had stacked a small neat pile of firewood, and he was now carrying an armload into the house. "You'll need more, but this should do you for a night or two."

She stepped aside to let him enter. He went straight to the fireplace and began arranging paper, kindling and logs for a fire. She glanced outside and saw that Chris, still wearing the Walkman, had dropped down on a big flat stump. He was clearly exhausted.

"That ought to do it," Ben said, getting up. "I believe you may even survive the night." He paused, then added, "If your husband's joining you, he can chop some more for you."

Jenny froze. "No one is joining me," she said.

"Oh." His look sized her up again. "Well, then we'll figure out some other way."

For a moment his dark eyes lingered on her face. "How's the headache? Any better?"

"What headache?"

"The one that put those lines in your forehead."

Jenny's fingers flew to her forehead. Then she shoved both hands into the back pockets of her jeans. "I'm fine," she said.

"It's no big deal," he said. "Everybody looks that way when they first get here for the summer. It's the city look. Boston, in your case, right?" His eyes went to the Celtics logo on her sweatshirt.

Jenny ignored the question. "Thank you for your help," she said stiffly. "I'm sure we'll be able to manage all right from here on."

"Oh, you will," he agreed, and now his voice took on a sardonic edge. "Once you get electricity and hot water and a telephone and can hook up that TV you brought, you won't even know you've left home."

"Have you something against being comfortable?" she demanded, wondering how he knew about the television set. She hadn't wanted to bring it, but Chris had insisted.

"Depends on your definition of comfort, I guess," he said, turning and walking toward the door. "I brought you a couple of kerosene lamps," he added over his shoulder.

"Thank you," she murmured again. He strode out, letting the screen door bang shut behind him and waving at Chris as he passed the stump where the boy was sitting. "So long, kid. Be seeing you."

Chris raised one hand, but said nothing. Ben called the two dogs, climbed into the truck and roared off. Despite everything, she was sorry to see him go, reluctant to have the stillness settle in around her with her silent resentful son her only company. She pressed her fingers to her temples, willing the throbbing to go away.

By six o'clock she had managed to wash the big windows facing the lake. The sun hung lower now, and she thought there might be a spectacular sunset. She wanted Chris to see it. She remembered herself as a small girl watching sunsets from this room. They'd have plenty of time to drive into town for some fast food and still get back for it.

When she heard the sound of an engine coming closer and then stopping, her heart did an unaccountable flip-flop. Ben Sullivan? What had he come back for? She hurried to the back door.

Instead of the pickup, however, it was an old dented Plymouth. A woman got out. She was wearing blue jeans and an untucked flowered shirt. She was thin as a rail, and her frizzy gray hair reminded Jenny of steel wool.

"Mrs. Carver? I'm Adele Hazelton. Heard what happened to you, so I thought I'd run in with something to tide you over."

Jenny's mind scurried over the possibilities. Had Ben Sullivan told this woman about her, or was she simply someone else who'd been part of the Tucker's Pond telegraph system?

"I know what it's like to have your stove not working," the woman said, yanking at a large basket in the back seat. "Time we had Hurricane Bob up here that happened to me, because mine was electric. Kids just about drove me crazy, and I'll tell you, we all got sick of peanut-butter sandwiches. You've got a boy, too, haven't you?"

"Yes. Yes, I have," Jenny said, glancing around as if looking for him. "He's here somewhere."

"Oh, kids." Adele carried the basket to the house. "Minute you get 'em out in the woods they just run wild. Don't know what to do first."

Jenny smiled and nodded, thinking of Chris, whom she had left moments ago, sitting on the edge of his bed, still listening to music through the headphones and biting his nails. She held the screen door open and Adele came in and deposited the basket on the long harvest table in the main room. She gave Jenny a sideways glance.

"I remember you, you know," she said.

"You do?" Jenny found this surprising. Twelve years was a long time.

"Sure. Remember you coming up here summers with your mother and father. I used to bring stuff over from my garden. Your daddy was partial to my tomatoes."

"I do remember some awfully good tomatoes," Jenny said.

"I felt real bad when I heard about your mother's passing."

Jenny nodded, not answering.

"Now we see your father and the other lady he married. She seems very nice." She paused slightly. "Quite a while since you've been here, though."

"I've been busy," Jenny murmured.

"Yep. That's the way it goes." Adele turned to the basket she'd brought. "Well now," she said. "I didn't have time to do anything fancy. It's just a chicken pie and a few homemade biscuits. There's a thermos of coffee for you and some milk for your boy. And some of my chocolate layer cake for dessert." She was lifting the things out as she spoke. Spread on the table, it looked like a feast.

"I don't know how to thank you," Jenny said. "That was such a thoughtful thing to do."

Adele Hazelton appeared surprised. "It's nothing much," she said. "We all try to do for each other when there's a need."

A masterpiece of understatement, Jenny thought. "I'll be sure to get the dishes back to you," she promised.

Adele waved a hand dismissively. "Oh, Ben Sullivan can bring 'em to me. He'll be stopping in to be sure your pump's working and your propane's hooked up." She glanced around. "I guess you'll be snug enough tonight."

"Won't you sit for a minute?" Jenny asked.

"Oh, thanks, Mrs. Carver, but I'd better be getting home. My kids'll be waiting for their supper."

"Please call me Jenny."

"Well, then, Jenny. Glad you're here. Hope we see more of you. I live on Radford Road if you need anything."

After Adele was gone, clanking off in the old Plymouth, Jenny began to set the table. A few minutes later, Chris appeared, his ears at last free of headphones. He stared at the table.

"I thought we were going into town to get pizza," he said. His voice held complaint.

Jenny breathed deeply, determined to remain patient.

"Well, I thought so, too, but a very kind woman brought this wonderful food for us, so now we don't have to."

He eyed it suspiciously. "What is all that stuff?"

"Chicken pie, homemade rolls. Chocolate cake."

"Is there soda?"

"No, but she brought milk."

Chris rolled his eyes. As they sat down to eat, he gestured insolently at the chicken pie.

"What's in that?"

"Oh…chicken, vegetables, lots of different things."
Watching him poke at it with his fork, she tried to distract him. "I thought maybe we could get the canoe out tomorrow and go for a paddle around the lake."

"I don't know how to work a canoe."

"You don't really have to work it at all. It's easy. I'll show you."

"I don't know if I want to do that."

Jenny felt irritation rising. "What do you want to do, then?"

His thin shoulders went up in a shrug. "If we get electricity, I can hook up the TV set."

Jenny made no reply, but went on eating. The food was too delicious to spoil with arguments, and even Chris finally settled down and ate without any more complaints.

He left the table as soon as he was finished, however, and returned to his bedroom. Jenny stacked the dishes in the kitchen sink and went down to the lake with the bucket. Sunset was still a half hour away, she judged, but with the remaining clouds low on the horizon, it would be worth seeing.

She brought water back, rinsed the dishes and then left them soaking in the sink. She found another pail, this one a galvanized metal one, and returned to the lake for more water. She could feel coolness creeping into the air already. If she lighted a fire, she could leave the bucket near it and the water would warm enough for them to wash up before bed.

"Chris? Come and look at the sun going down," she called as she came in. She thought he probably hadn't heard her, but in a minute he came out of his room and joined her. He looked pale and tired and bored. She pointed out through the big windows at the colors spreading across the sky and reflecting off the lake, rose and gold streaked here and there with lavender.

"Isn't it beautiful?"

"Yeah."

"I thought we'd have a fire. Wouldn't that be fun?"

"I guess."

She found matches in the kitchen and ignited the kindling Ben Sullivan had arranged. The light was fading fast, the air turning chilly. The leaping flames were cheerful and lively. Chris watched them for a few minutes, but then turned away restlessly and went to his room. Jenny sat by the fire, wishing she could think of things to say to him, words that would bring them close, so that they would then understand each other, and he would look to her for love and guidance, as he had when he was little.

When she climbed into bed later, her head was still throbbing, and she could feel the massive headache coming closer. *Aspirin,* she thought. *I'd better take some now.* She sat up, trying to remember where the tablets were. She hadn't even finished unpacking. She'd brought drinking water in from the kitchen, but she'd forgotten a flashlight. Something else she'd have to buy tomorrow. Suddenly it all seemed like more than she could handle. Not only the headache and finding the aspirin, but the whole month stretching ahead of her. She'd made a major mistake. How was she going to get through it? What was she going to do with Chris? But if they went back to Boston, how would that be any better? There'd been trouble there, too. Suddenly, not realizing she was doing it, she reached up with one hand to touch her forehead. She could feel the tense lines there. She fell back on the pillow and began to sob quietly.

She'd left the bedroom window partially open. The night air coming in was chilly but fresh. Jenny pulled the blankets up and lay huddled under them wretchedly. Suddenly from far away she heard music. She grew quiet, her sobbing tapering off as she listened. Where was it coming from? A house somewhere along the lake? Probably a few of the summer people were here already. She lay quietly, trying to identify the music. Just when she thought she recognized it, it escaped her. But it kept rising and falling gently, melody running in and out in soothing patterns, and after a time she could feel the throbbing in her temples starting to ease. Her arms and legs began to relax. She uncurled from her tight position and stretched luxuriously, smelling the piney fragrance of the night woods, listening to the distant music, never knowing when she fell asleep.

CHAPTER TWO

WHEN SHE WOKE in the morning, Jenny discovered she had pulled the blankets up around her ears, but she felt clearheaded and rested. She got up, looking out through her window into the woods and on down to the lake, which lay shrouded in gray mist. From somewhere over the water she could hear the cry of a loon. She went to the bureau for her watch. Almost seven. She tiptoed out and glanced into Chris's room. He was sleeping soundly, and he, too, had tugged the covers up around him.

Jenny hurried back to her room and pulled on her jeans and sweatshirt, shivering a little in the early-morning chill. Then she went through the kitchen and slipped outside. The woods around her smelled tangy and fresh. All trace of her headache had disappeared. To the right she could glimpse the small guest house through the trees. She would explore that later, she decided. She walked out along the driveway to the curve. Just beyond that it branched off to the left and continued into the woods. There were more summer properties out that way as well as some year-round houses occupied by local people. She even remembered one of their names. Howell. She remembered Mrs. Howell giving her cookies when she was little. Jenny and her mother had walked there together, hand in hand.

Moved by a sudden thought, Jenny returned to the house and located a mug and a jar of instant coffee. She put a spoonful of coffee into the mug and went back outside. The Howells might be long gone, but who could tell? Somebody must live there. And if they were as kind as Adele Hazelton, they might be willing to give her some boiling water for coffee. It was early, but she knew people in this part of the world started their days early.

The house, when she reached it, looked different. She remembered white, and this had a natural wood finish. Also, it looked larger, as if something had been added in back. She went to the door and knocked softly. A dog barked. Then a second joined in. Jenny had a moment's terrible misgiving.

The door was thrust open. Ben Sullivan stood there barefoot, wearing jeans but no shirt, his hair slightly rumpled. For a second they looked at each other. The two dogs crowded around his feet.

"Oh, I *am* sorry," Jenny said. "That is, I didn't realize you lived here. I thought..." She found herself staring at his bare chest and the flat tapering look of his waist.

One of his dark eyebrows went up. "Tired of roughing it already?"

Jenny swallowed. "I'm afraid I just can't rough it without coffee. I was hoping to find someone who wouldn't mind putting some boiling water into my mug."

He peered into the mug in question. "That's instant," he said critically. "Why don't we make some real coffee?" It wasn't the warmest of welcomes, but he stood back and held the door open for her. She stepped inside, glancing around a big open room lined with bookshelves and furnished with chairs and couches that looked inviting.

"Kitchen's out here," he said, leading the way to a spacious room with big windows, a good-size wooden table and weathered-looking cabinets. All the appliances appeared new and well cared for.

"Really, just some boiling water would do." Suddenly she felt very self-conscious. If there was a wife about to appear, what would she think of Jenny's showing up so brashly? But he'd left the kitchen. When he returned he had put on a sweatshirt and slipped his feet into worn deck shoes. Had she wakened him? No, she decided, she could see he'd already shaved.

"I was going to make coffee, anyway," he said, and started measuring grounds into the filter. "How'd you sleep?"

"Wonderfully," she said, hesitating briefly and then sliding into a chair at the table. The black dog crawled under it and flopped down near her feet. The other one stayed back in a corner, his nose resting on his paws but his eyes taking in every movement. "A very nice woman named Adele brought us food, which helped a lot. And then just as I was trying to sleep I heard music coming from somewhere." She stopped short and looked back through the open archway into the big main room. A stereo system was built into shelves on the wall between the two front windows. "Was that you?"

"Sorry. Did it disturb you?" He poured water into the coffeemaker.

"Oh, no. In fact, it put me to sleep."

"Then the headache's better, I take it."

"Completely gone."

"Good. You may survive, after all." He moved to a cupboard and returned with muffins. "These were made by Adele, who now and then takes pity on me, too. She's an ace baker."

"Does she keep house for you?" Jenny was looking around, still thinking nervously about a wife. The house had a casual, lived-in look, but it was clean and orderly despite that.

"No, I'm my own housekeeper. Adele and her husband are just good friends of mine." He sat down opposite her. "I guess I was a little tough on you yesterday," he said. "It was a busy day for me and I was trying to work everything in. City people have a way of wanting things done right away."

It was an apology of sorts, but no smile went with it. Jenny had a feeling "city people" didn't bring out the best in Ben Sullivan.

After a moment he got up and went to pour coffee for both of them. When he handed her a cup, she took a sip, finding it dark and strong. She hesitated for a moment and then said, "I know what you must have been thinking." His look turned curious. She went on slowly, "You were thinking I was a spoiled young woman from Boston with a rich father. Used to having my own way and fit to be tied because there wasn't any hot water, not to mention ice cubes for my Perrier."

"Well...that's close, isn't it?" Both black eyebrows went up this time as he regarded her over the rim of his cup.

Jenny returned his look. "Do you want to hear what my week was really like?" She took another sip, then put her cup down. "I work for a law firm in Boston— as a paralegal—and they only told me at the last minute that I could have this month off, which'll be my first vacation in three years. I had to slave like mad to get all my work finished so I could leave. And last Wednesday I completed my night courses in contract law and took my exam. It was a killer, but I got through it, though I don't know if I passed yet. Then I had to call my father, whom I haven't talked to in about five years. It was awkward, but I wanted to come up here with Chris. Not just because I have good memories from when I was young, but because it's the only place I could possibly afford. If my father and his wife had been planning to be up here, I wouldn't have come. But it worked out." Pausing for breath, Jenny could scarcely believe she'd told such personal things to a man she didn't know.

She lowered her gaze, and for a while he said nothing, but she could feel him watching her. Then he said slowly, "You're right. That's not the picture I had of you."

"Well, now you know."

"How come you punish yourself that way? I mean, working that hard."

"I have to support myself and Chris. I want to do something with my life."

"There are other things you could do."

"And I've done a lot of them. Waitressing, making beds in motels, clerking in a department store. I've never had anybody to depend on but myself."

"You had a husband once."

She brushed the idea away with a motion of her hand. "We were kids. Just graduated from high school. My mother had died a few months before, my father was grieving so he hardly spoke to me. I needed . . . somebody, I guess. Anyway, it lasted about five minutes. Okay, six months—we were divorced before Chris was born." She added wryly, "My father took that whole episode very personally. He never forgave me—or Chris for being born. I made a stab at keeping in touch for a few years, but it wasn't working."

And just as she'd lost all the ties to her own father, she thought, Chris had no connection with his—that young husband whose face Jenny could scarcely recall now. It bothered her, Chris's having no male influence in his life. But of course there was Philip....

The room was silent for a few moments while Jenny felt a slow creeping horror at having divulged so much of her personal history to a complete stranger. What had gotten into her, anyway? She sipped her coffee and kept her eyes away from him.

He said, "So now you're on the fast track." He was giving her a look of assessment. "How's it working out? I mean, you say you're doing it for your son. How is it for him?"

Jenny could feel an all-too-familiar anxiety as she struggled for the right words to answer him. "It isn't always easy, if that's what you mean. But once I have my law degree and pass the bar exam, I'm pretty sure there'll be a place for me in the firm I work for. I'll be making better money, and things will be a lot easier for us." There was more, of course, but she'd already said too much. She wasn't going to talk to him about Philip and what their plans might be.

"And then your daddy will realize that you really do amount to something," he said lazily. His eyes skimmed over her.

Jenny tried to keep her voice pleasant, but it still came out with a slight edge. "That's none of your business, you know."

He spread both hands. "You brought it up."

"I never said—"

"No, but if you and he haven't spoken in five years, it doesn't take a rocket scientist to figure out you aren't exactly buddies. Anyway, you said so yourself. Why be so stiff-necked? He could have helped you."

"I really don't want to talk about it."

"Okay, okay," he said, raising a hand in a defensive motion. "Change of subject. I called the power company yesterday just before they closed. They'll be out at your place today. Also the phone company and the propane people. I'll stop over later and turn things on in the pump house."

"Thank you." She spoke in a low voice, and another silence fell between them. Outside, birds were tuning up for the day, and sunlight was beginning to break through the mist. Ben Sullivan didn't seem bothered by the pause in the conversation. He finished his coffee and got up to pour more for both of them.

When he was seated again, Jenny said softly, "I thought it would be good for Chris to be here. When I was twelve, coming to Tucker's Pond was a magical thing. My mother was alive then. In fact, we used to walk through the woods to this house. An old lady lived here."

"Mrs. Howell."

"She gave me cookies, I remember."

He nodded. "I bought the house when she died." Then he said, "Is that what Chris is—twelve?"

"Yes."

"He looks older. I'd have thought fifteen."

"Well, he's tall. Maybe that's it." But there was more to it than that. The old-beyond-his-years look he wore, the boredom in his face. She longed to see the wide-eyed excitement, the wonder of childhood in him, but there was only that world-weary expression, and so often, lately, a kind of furtiveness that troubled her.

"Yes, that could be it," he said.

"Well, I'd better be going," she said. "Maybe I'll take Chris a muffin, if you don't mind."

"Take all you want."

"Thanks. One will do. We'll have to go into town and stock up today." She wrapped the muffin in a paper napkin, pushed back her chair and stood up. At the scraping sound, the brindle dog leapt up from the corner and, growling low in its throat, took a menacing step toward her. Jenny gave a start and stumbled against the table. At once Ben Sullivan was on his feet and his arms were around her, steadying her.

"Blaze! That'll do! Sit!" The dog instantly retreated.

Jenny felt a jolt of sensual response in herself that shocked her. His were such strong capable arms, so comforting and protective.

"I'm sorry," he said. "Blaze isn't the best with people." He released her slowly. "Are you okay?"

"Yes, of course." Jenny could feel the hot color in her own face. "I guess he's a good watchdog."

"I suppose, although that's not why I have him. I found him in the woods. Discarded by some summer people. He was half-wild when I brought him home. He's improved a lot, but he's not exactly sociable. Sure you're all right?"

"Absolutely." She started for the door, giving Blaze a wide berth. The dog followed her with his eyes.

"I'll be over later," he said. "To see that your hotwater heater's working."

"Thank you. I really appreciate it." She felt an unfamiliar shyness because he'd touched her, an acute awareness of his powerful male presence.

Walking back to the cabin along the narrow drive, it occurred to her that he hadn't smiled once during the time she was there. And he hadn't told her a thing about himself. He knew a great deal about her now, but she knew absolutely nothing about him except that he had once brought home a half-wild dog and adopted it. Ben Sullivan seemed the sort of man who wanted to remain by himself in his snug house in the pines. And the less he had to do with society, the better he liked it. Rather like that dog of his, she thought.

Yet the surprising strength of his arms around her, the immediate thrill she'd felt through her body, kept returning to her. It had been a long time since she'd reacted like that to a man's touch.

Chris, when she handed him the muffin, ate it with gratifying speed. At least his appetite had improved here.

"Where'd you get this?" he mumbled through crumbs.

"At Ben Sullivan's," she said. "I took a walk through the woods earlier. Why didn't you tell me he lived so near? That's where you went for the firewood, isn't it?"

"Yeah. I mean, I guess. I wasn't paying attention."

Trucks began arriving then, and in rapid succession the power was hooked up, propane was delivered, and the telephone was restored, so that its comforting dial tone purred once again. Afterward, Jenny and Chris drove to town for a late breakfast at a fast-food restaurant and a trip to the local supermarket. Jenny weakened to the extent of laying in a supply of frozen pizzas for Chris, hoping it would help to break through his sullen silence, but he remained uncommunicative. When they returned, Ben Sullivan's truck was parked by the house. Jenny's heart jumped.

Chris paid no attention to it. "I'm going to set up the TV," he announced. He'd lugged the set in from the car the night before.

"Here—take some of these groceries on your way."

When he was gone, she began to unload the rest of the things, keeping one eye on the little pump house halfway down the slope toward the dock. Presently Ben Sullivan emerged, caught sight of her and gave a nod.

"Pump seems to be working fine. I oiled it and checked it over. We'd better go in and try the faucets. Let me give you a hand with those."

He took two of the heavy bags from her, and she followed him into the house. His stride was long and easy, and he carried the bags as if they were weightless. Once inside, they went through the business of turning on faucets, listening to the hiss and spurt as air was pushed out and finally, satisfyingly, watching the gush of water. In the bathroom, where the hot-water tank stood, he turned on the heating unit.

"Won't take long," he said. "You'll have hot water in a few minutes."

"Thank you so much," she said. His nearness was again disturbing her. The house seemed a different place with him in it—more alive, more vital. He became its center simply by being there.

"On my way out I'll lift the canoe down from the rack in the shed," he said. "You and the boy might want to use it."

"I can help," she said.

"No need," he said, and she nodded, feeling rebuffed. From the bedroom came the sound of a television set blaring and squawking as Chris changed channels. Ben heard it, too, and he turned that way briefly, but made no comment.

She watched from the doorway as he went to the shed and carried the canoe down to the lake, tying it fast to a cleat on the dock. Then, without another look toward the house, he vaulted easily into the truck and took off.

A heavy gray cloud of loneliness seemed to settle around Jenny. He'd done everything that needed doing, so it wasn't likely she'd have occasion to see him again. Just as well. It was impossible to mistake his disapproval of her. He didn't like her, her life-style or the way she was raising her son. Another person criticizing her was not exactly what she needed at the moment. Taking a deep breath, she went off in search of a bucket, cleaning rags and detergent.

For the next hour she worked hard at scrubbing the refrigerator, sink, stove, putting away groceries and checking cupboards to see what staple items were on hand. She made a mental note to replace anything she used before they went home. The shelves were neat and orderly, everything in place. She'd never met her father's second wife, Grace, whom he'd married less than two years ago. Jenny had simply received a cool, impersonal announcement of the event. She'd formed a picture of someone efficient, quick to pick up bits of lint and carry off empty coffee cups. Jenny had re-

ceived brief notes from her during the early days of the
marriage, but had sent only minimal replies, and now
all that came was a Christmas card.

"What's for lunch?" Chris asked, coming into the
kitchen just as she was finishing.

"Didn't we just eat?"

"It's one o'clock," he said.

They made sandwiches and carried them to the table in the main room. "How about a swim later?"
Jenny asked.

"I tried the water. It's cold."

"We could go out in the canoe. Ben Sullivan got it
ready for us."

The boy's thin shoulders lifted in a shrug. "Maybe
I'll just watch TV."

"But you can do that at home," she said, trying not
to sound exasperated. "It's really beautiful out on the
lake."

"Big deal," he muttered, and went back to his room.
As he shut the door, Jenny slumped forward, her elbows on the table, her head in her hands.

Later she walked along the path through ferns and
towering trees to the small log guest house. She'd found
the key hanging in the kitchen. She could see as she
opened the door that it had been done in a simple style,
much like the main house, with knotty-pine walls and
braided rugs scattered on the floor. There were two
rooms and a bath, one of the rooms furnished with
twin beds, the other apparently used at the moment for
storage, given the piles of stacked cartons. The place
had a homey, comfortable look.

She walked around the storage room. One of the
cartons was labeled "Books." Jenny lifted the flap to
peek inside and saw on top her old worn copies of *Lit-*

tle Women and *Winnie the Pooh*. She opened another carton. This time her own name caught her eye, but it was on a large, unfamiliar scrapbook. She lifted it out carefully. Not a scrapbook, she realized, but a photograph album. She opened it and felt a sudden pang as her own face looked back at her. A youthful Jenny, her smile glinting with braces, her legs too long for the rest of her, hair yanked back in a ponytail. And even older pictures—herself as a toddler, holding her mother's hand. Tears sprang to her eyes as she looked at it. Another picture showed her being held in the arms of a handsome young man with an unmistakable profile— her father. Jenny closed the album quickly, finding it too painful to look at. Who could possibly have made it? Her father? It seemed an uncharacteristically sentimental thing for Buzz Carmichael to do.

She went into the other room and sank down on the edge of one of the beds. After a moment she lifted her feet up and lay back wearily. For a long time she stayed there, drifting in and out of sleep, while strange and disturbing images kept recurring to her. Ben Sullivan's piercing dark eyes and black eyebrows, his broad bare chest, the unsmiling yet sensual line of his mouth. A young, lanky Jenny with shining braces. Presently, with an effort, she roused herself. She should go back. Perhaps Chris could be coaxed into a walk, at least.

As she closed the door and started toward the main house, she paused and listened. She heard voices. Whose? She moved along the path quietly, looking through the trees toward the lake, where the sound seemed to be coming from. And suddenly, through an opening, she saw two figures standing on the dock. The taller one seemed to be doing the talking. It was Ben Sullivan, and Chris was with him. Both of them were holding fishing rods. Farther out on the dock the two dogs snoozed. Jenny stood still. Words and snatches of sentences drifted to her.

"Keep your wrist stiff... You have to control the line... See, like this..."

Jenny moved a little nearer.

"The best fly fishermen say that how you cast reflects who you are. It's a personal thing. But you still have to master the basics. Try it again."

Astonished, Jenny watched as the boy pulled his arm back and made an awkward cast that dribbled into the water a few feet in front of him.

"Much better," she heard Sullivan say. "You're getting the hang of it. But wait for the line to straighten out behind you before you start it forward."

Chris turned to ask something that Jenny couldn't hear.

He answered, "Well, I've seen plenty of bass around your dock here, and that's a fly they usually go for. It's called a gray ghost."

Chris said something else and Ben replied, "Sure, you can buy them, but the best ones are the ones you make. These are my own."

"You *made* these things?" This time Jenny could hear Chris's astonished voice plainly.

"Sure. Try it again now. It should hit like a real fly landing on the water. Got to fool the fish, see. And don't bend that wrist."

Jenny walked slowly through the trees toward the dock. They were too preoccupied to notice her at first. Then the brindle dog let out a low growl, and they both looked around. Chris, intent on what he was doing, gave Jenny only a cursory glance. Ben Sullivan's eyes lingered on her in that unsmiling way she found so unsettling.

"I don't think I'll ever make a friend of that dog," she said lightly.

"Blaze, quiet," Ben ordered. He kept his gaze on her. "I meant to ask you this morning for permission to use your dock now and then. It slipped my mind. I'm afraid I'm used to sneaking over here, since my place isn't on the water. Usually there's no one around to care."

"It's perfectly all right," she said. Inwardly, however, she was experiencing a strange mix of emotions. The concentration she saw in Chris was a surprise. His obviously genuine effort to master the art of fly casting astonished her, and she knew she should be grateful to Ben Sullivan for taking time with the boy. How had he ever pried him away from the TV? Yet at the same time, it was obvious that he thought she was doing a poor job of raising her son and felt sorry for him. He was trying that good old male-bonding thing, probably so sure he could straighten everything out with a few minutes with a fishing rod. Well, Chris did need that, didn't he? she argued with herself. He'd never had contact with his father or his father's family, who had disapproved of the marriage from the beginning. And certainly her own father had never reached out a hand to him.

Chris made another cast, slightly less awkward.

"You're getting there," Ben assured him.

"Mom, look in that box," Chris said. "Look at all those things he made."

She picked up the flat box, which was clear plastic and sectioned off into compartments. In spite of herself she caught her breath as she looked at the flies.

They were delicate little creations of floss and feathers and tinsel, some of them winged, each one a tiny work of art.

"Every one's got a name," Chris told her.

"Really."

"That one you're holding is a Parmachene belle," Ben said. He took a step over to her and pointed with a long tanned finger. "That's a muddler minnow and that one's a woolyworm."

"What wonderful names." She was watching the finger now and beginning to feel a curious warmth stealing over her. His presence was like a tangible force that she reacted to, her body going in one direction and her mind in another. She watched as Chris cast once more. His awkwardness around the house drove her to distraction more often than not, but here he was actually starting to take on a look of capability. Man triumphs over woman again, she thought wryly.

"Hey!" Chris's voice held surprise and excitement. "Hey, what's that?"

Ben turned away from her and observed the tug on the boy's line. "You've got yourself a bite."

"A fish? I've caught a fish?"

"Well, you haven't caught him yet, but things are looking pretty good. Bring him in slowly now, no sudden jerks. You don't want him to throw the hook."

Jenny stood back, watching as Ben Sullivan stood behind Chris, coaching and encouraging. Then she sighed. Who was she to complain if he helped Chris?

She stayed on the dock, observing quietly as the afternoon shadows lengthened. She admired the bass Chris caught, watched as he and Ben continued casting. When at last Ben caught a fish he said, "There. That'll do."

"Aren't we going to fish anymore?" Chris sounded disappointed.

"Not today," Ben said. "Those two are plenty for your supper. First rule—never catch more than you can eat. If you do, you have to put them back in the water."

"Is that the law?" the boy asked. "You have to throw them back?"

"Sullivan's Law," he said. "And you never throw them. You release them gently. Now, let's get busy and clean these."

Jenny regarded the fish. "There's more than enough for the two of us." She hesitated. "Maybe you'd like to stay and help eat them."

"Yeah, how about that?" Chris asked.

"Okay," Ben said. "Sure." His eyes met Jenny's and held for a moment.

Feeling unaccountably flustered, she said, "I'll go see what else I can scare up. We can use the outdoor grill. I bought charcoal today."

His voice followed her as she went up the path toward the house. She heard him tell Chris, "You hold the knife like this and take the scales off by scraping from the tail to the head. Then hold it this way...."

In the end, it was Ben who did most of the cooking. He sliced potatoes with their skins on and cooked them in foil on the grill with onions, butter and plenty of black pepper. The fish, cleaned and filleted, went on the grill, too. Jenny prepared a salad.

"Shall we eat outside?" she asked when everything was ready.

He shook his head. "You've forgotten how quickly the evenings turn cold around here." He gave a quick glance at the sky. "This looks like a forties night to me. We'd do better to go inside and start a fire."

Chris, who had scarcely uttered a complete sentence since Jenny had brought him to Maine, was full of questions as they ate.

"How'd you learn all that stuff about fishing?"

"Well, I grew up in Maine."

"But somebody must've taught you."

"My dad, mostly. And my grandfather."

"Did he know about it, too?"

"Oh, yes. Granddad knew everything there was to know about the woods and the lakes and the country around here."

Jenny sat back, looking from one to the other but not interrupting, eating with an appetite she didn't know she had, savoring the delicacy of the fresh-caught fish and tender potatoes.

When they were finished, Chris pulled on a sweatshirt and went down to the dock with Rocket at his heels. Presently there were sounds of the dog splashing into the water after sticks.

Jenny and Ben sat at the table watching the sun set lavishly over the lake. Jenny could feel herself unwinding, all her nerves stretching out loosely.

"That's a very satisfied look," he observed. His almost black eyes were studying her. Jenny could see sparks of firelight reflected in them.

She said hesitantly, "I was just thinking—we've been here a little over twenty-four hours and this is the first time I've felt really relaxed. I mean, right now the office and Boston and contract law seem as far away as Mars."

For the first time she saw a faint smile playing at the corners of his mouth.

"Life in the slow lane has its good points," he said. "This place will do that to you if you give it a chance."

"Well, of course," she admitted. "For a month or so."

"A month or so?" His black eyebrows rose. "It takes a month or so just to pick up the rhythm of the place."

"I feel pretty lucky to have that much time," she said. "Working in the city, it isn't often that—"

"There's a moose, for instance," he interrupted. "Occasionally he comes in the evening to drink from the lake right near here. In a month you might not even get a look at him. It could take all summer."

"Well, that would be lovely, but..." Her voice trailed off and then she added, "It's very isolated up here. I mean, it must be, especially during the rest of the year. Aren't you ever lonely?"

The question hung in the air, the room silent except for the crackling of the fire. She became aware of the assessing look he was giving her.

"I've never thought about it much," he said quietly. "Until now."

Jenny looked back at him, unable to tear her gaze away. Then a loud whoop from the direction of the water gave her an excuse to break eye contact. She got up and stepped out onto the narrow porch, hearing Ben follow close behind her.

Rocket, it seemed, had just climbed onto the dock and shaken water in all directions. Chris was on his knees wrestling playfully with the dog, the two of them an indistinguishable mass of boy and dog. Back on the shore, the wary Blaze crouched and watched.

Jenny said, without turning to Ben, "Thank you."

"For what?" His voice was near. She could feel his breath against her hair.

"For today," she said. "For showing Chris how to fish. For cooking our dinner. It's done him so much good."

"You're welcome," he said. "I had a good time, too. And for Pete's sake, every boy should know how to fly cast."

He caught her by the shoulders and turned her to face him. His eyes moved over her features slowly, and then he bent to kiss her. The touch of his lips was so light that she felt herself leaning into it, wishing for more. But he pulled away and said in his matter-of-fact voice, "I'd better be going."

"Will you come again? I know Chris would love it."

"I'll be around," he said noncommittally.

Would he? Jenny wondered as she cleared away the dishes. She had the distinct impression that he'd had second thoughts the moment his lips touched hers. Ben Sullivan seemed a man who shied away from involvement. Well, that simplified things. The last thing she needed was some silly summer flirtation. Her life was complicated enough.

Yet the suspicion lurked in the back of her mind that nothing about Ben was silly, and a summer flirtation was the last thing a woman would have with him.

CHAPTER THREE

JENNY KNEW the minute she opened her eyes the next morning, that she had overslept. Light was streaming into the pine-walled bedroom and the birds outside were already noisy. Back in Boston, she would have leapt up guiltily. Here what the clock said seemed less important, and she allowed herself a few blissful moments of snuggling back into the warm cocoon of the covers. The morning air was crisp and still cool. Almost at once she saw again the scene on the narrow porch the night before, felt the light touch of Ben Sullivan's kiss. A friendly kiss, she thought. Was there really such a thing between a man and a woman? If it had been no more than friendly, why did the memory of it start such a tumult of reactions in her body?

She heard a rhythmic pounding and lay perfectly still, trying to identify it. It was coming from outside and voices were mixed with it. She pushed back the covers and tiptoed to the open window. At the edge of the clearing Ben Sullivan and Chris were chopping wood and stacking it. After the first sudden leap of her heart, parental anxiety crowded in. Chris was too young to be working with something as dangerous as an ax. He didn't know how to handle it; he'd hurt himself. But she didn't move to call out.

"My granddad always used to say that good wood warms you twice," Ben was saying. "Once when you chop it and once when you burn it."

"It sure is cold up here at night," Chris said.

"Yeah, I figured we'd better build this pile up a little. If you're going to be here a month, you'll need it."

"Did your grandfather know how to make those things you showed me?"

"The flies, you mean? Sure. He taught me. I've still got some of his stuff. His vise, for one."

"What's that?"

"It's a clamp you use to hold the fly while you're working on it."

Chips flew. The air was scented with the smell of the fresh-cut wood. A short distance away Rocket watched lazily while Blaze sat among the bracken, his eyes following the strokes of the axes. The reality of Chris's being up early without her coaxing and threatening suddenly hit Jenny.

"Hold the ax farther back, toward the end of the handle," Ben ordered. "You want it to do the work, not you. And never take your eyes off what you're doing. You have to learn to respect the power of tools."

Jenny saw Chris adjust his grip.

"That's better. Now that piece has a knot in it. See it there? Don't try to chop through it—it's apt to make your ax bounce off. Go to one side of it."

"Okay." There was another blow of the ax, then another thunk as the log was tossed onto a growing pile. "How about that big one?"

"We need the wedge and maul for that. Have to split it first. Try to position the wedge right about dead center—"

"Good morning!" Jenny called from the window. They turned to her, and the morning light caught Ben's black hair and outlined the breadth of his shoulders under his plaid shirt.

"Well! About time." He grinned. His smile was still so unfamiliar to her that it was a source of wonder.

"Has anybody had breakfast?" she asked a little breathlessly.

"I have, but my assistant here's been complaining."

"Yeah, Mom, how about some food?"

"Give me five minutes."

She hurried through a shower and dressed hastily in jeans, faded blue shirt and a bright red sweater. In the kitchen, she got out orange juice, cereal and milk, started the coffee, then went to the door and waved the wood choppers in.

While Chris attacked a bowl of cereal, Jenny made toast and poured coffee for Ben.

"You must have worked up an appetite again," she said, putting toast and marmalade in front of him. She'd felt his eyes following her around the kitchen.

"Not a serious one, but I can manage this," he said.

"How did you two wind up out there so early?" she asked, sitting down with her own coffee. She turned to Chris. "Did you plan it last night?"

He nodded, shoveling in cereal and reaching for toast.

"Ben said we'd be needing more wood and he'd be over early with it, that's all."

"And you woke up by yourself?"

"Sure."

Ben glanced at the boy. "He set his internal clock."

Jenny shook her head. "School never seems to activate that clock."

Both of them shrugged, shoulders going up in the same way. Jenny burst out laughing. Chris wiped his mouth with his napkin and stood up. "I'm gonna go outside," he said.

"Wait till I come out before you do any more chopping," Ben said.

"Okay. I just want to throw some sticks for Rocket. She's waiting for me."

He banged out through the screen door. Jenny got up to pour more coffee, and Ben asked, "Does it worry you, his working with the ax?"

She was amazed that he had read her thoughts so accurately. She poured the coffee and sat down again.

"It surprised me a little," she said, not wanting to make too much of it, despite her lingering anxiety. "He does seem a bit young to be doing such things."

There was silence between them. From down by the water they heard a splash and a shout.

"What kind of things does he do back in the city?" Ben asked quietly. "Aren't there some dangers there, too?"

Jenny looked down at the table. All the worries, all the misgivings, all the sleepless nights suddenly flooded over her. Dangers in the city. If he knew how often they'd overwhelmed her...

Again, Ben seemed to be in tune with her thoughts.

"There's danger everywhere," he said simply. "The only way to protect yourself from it is to be prepared—as much as anyone ever can be." He reached out and covered her hand on the table with his. "Chris'll be okay. He's a smart kid."

She nodded, trying to hold back the tears that were threatening.

"Don't worry so much," he said in a soft voice. "That's not what you came up here for, is it?"

She shook her head. "It's just that sometimes everything gets to be... too much. I have to do all the thinking for both of us. Make the decisions, try to manage. I'm afraid sometimes I wind up feeling pretty sorry for myself, and I hate that."

"You're entitled to it now and then," he said. "I told you yesterday—you're too hard on yourself. Besides, you're not to worry at Tucker's Pond. That's Sullivan's Second Law."

Jenny finally raised her eyes and managed a smile. He took his hand away, but the warmth of his touch lingered on her skin. She steered toward a safer subject. "Why do you suppose the lakes in Maine are called ponds?"

"Oh, a few of them are called lakes now," he said. "Which mostly happens when some go-getter decides it'd be better for the tourist trade. They think 'pond' sounds too hick. You watch, one of these days they'll try to rename Tucker's Pond something like Reflection Lake or Crystal Lake."

"Over your dead body?" Jenny suggested, laughing.

"Exactly." He pushed back his chair and got up. "I'd better get back to that woodpile. Have to finish stacking it so we can get to the rest of the program."

"Program?" Jenny gave him a questioning look.

He smiled down at her. "I promised Chris I'd show him a few of my grandfather's fly-tying techniques. After that he wants to learn something about canoeing."

Jenny laughed. "You sound like a camp counselor. What about your own work? You mustn't let Chris monopolize every minute of your time." She got up and began stacking dishes.

"I've decided to treat myself to a few days off," he said. "I've got all the houses in shape for the people who'll be here this month. Besides, it isn't entirely Chris who's doing the monopolizing."

She paused with a cup and saucer in her hand. "Really, I never meant to..." she began.

"I'm sure you didn't do it on purpose," he said, taking the cup and saucer from her and putting it down. He put both hands on her shoulders and looked at her. Dark fires glistened in his eyes as they searched her face. "It was just something about the way you looked yesterday, standing at my door with that damned coffee mug in your hand. You looked so..."

"Helpless?" she suggested wryly.

"No, never that. Appealing, I think. I'm not used to seeing that on my doorstep."

"Especially not at seven in the morning."

"It wouldn't matter what time it was," he murmured, and bent to kiss her. This time her lips parted in surprise, and she could feel her body melting against his. She was immediately aware that this was not the light, friendly kiss of the night before, but a plunge into some unknown territory they were exploring together. Her hands went around his neck; her fingers raked through his thick dark hair. Far back in her mind alarm bells sounded. What did she think she was doing? What was this thing she was embarking on with a man she knew almost nothing about? What about Philip? Jenny's lips moved softly under the passionate urging of his mouth. She closed her ears to the warning bells.

When Ben broke the kiss, he smiled and went outside. A short time later the wood was stacked to Ben's satisfaction, and he and Chris left. Not wanting to dwell on the kiss, Jenny flew around the house, making her bed, sweeping the floor and then washing a few clothes. Hanging them on the line outside, she felt as if she was playing house. Everything was so easy here, life reduced to its simplest elements. By the time Ben and Chris returned, she had made a stack of sandwiches.

"You both must be starving," she said. Seeing them walk in together made her heart pump with absurd joy.

"Can we wrap them up and take them with us?" Ben asked.

She was faintly disappointed, but hid it. "Sure," she said. "You're going to leave right away?"

"If you're ready."

"Me? I'm invited along on this trip?"

"Certainly."

Jenny felt another surge of joy, and it, too, was absurd, she told herself. This whole thing was unreal, but suddenly she didn't care. She had spent the past twelve years worrying about tomorrow, about managing, about doing the right thing. Now, she was going to do what her heart told her to.

Ben was looking at her with a smile, eyebrows lifted. "Well?"

"Ready when you are," Jenny said.

She sat in the center of the slender yellow canoe, with Chris in the bow and Ben in the stern.

"Just hold the paddle like this—here, and here. Lever it with your top hand as you go through the water, then give it a little twist like this as you pull it out."

"That's all?" asked Chris.

"That's all. Later on I'll teach you some stern strokes. If the blisters aren't too bad," he added with a grin.

"Where are we going?" Jenny asked.

Ben pointed to the right. "I thought we'd head up that way, toward the little beach that sticks out. We can eat our lunch there."

Jenny nodded and sat back happily. The sun was shining with midday strength, and she soon had to shed her red sweater. In front of her she could see her son's slender body bending to the unfamiliar motion of paddling. Behind her she could sense Ben's presence as he thrust the blade through the water with strong, sure strokes that sent the canoe skimming over the water. Once in a while he spoke quietly.

"Look off there to the right, in the shallows," he said, and Jenny saw what appeared to be a duck and twelve tiny ducklings.

"What are they?"

"Mergansers. And see the big tree at the edge of that point? Look at the top. That's an osprey's nest."

"It's huge!" Jenny said.

"That's because the ospreys use it year after year and every year they add to it. Can you make them out? I see one . . . maybe two."

"Are they ducks?" Chris asked.

"No—more like hawks. But like mergansers they live on fish."

"It seems to me there was an osprey's nest in that same tree when I was little," Jenny said.

They passed summer houses along the way, all discreetly back from the shore. A pair of loons landed on the water near them and swam along in their wake.

They beached the canoe on a small spit of land, climbed out and picnicked in the sunshine.

"Look! What's that?" Chris asked after a while.

"One of the ospreys doing a little fishing," Ben said, and they all watched as the big bird hovered, dived and came up with a fish. Powerful wings lifted him off the water, and he flew back to the treetop nest.

Chris rolled up his jeans and went wading in the shallows, wandering far off down the beach. Jenny folded her sweater into a pillow and lay back, eyes closed, listening to the sounds of the birds, the lapping of the water, the breeze stirring the branches of trees.

"I wouldn't have believed it," she murmured. Her eyes were closed, but she could feel Ben's nearness. He reached out and touched her hair, and she shivered inwardly.

"Wouldn't have believed what?"

"That I could be here like this today. Three days ago I was answering phones and looking up cases and running my legs off locating precedents and having trouble sleeping. It's another world entirely." She opened her eyes and found him propped up on one elbow beside her, studying her with those dark blue eyes. "I'm saving them," she said.

"Saving what?" His finger traced her forehead, her chin.

"These days. I won't forget any of them."

"Even that first one?"

"It wasn't so bad. Adele's food saved it." She turned her head slightly to watch Chris, who was now skipping stones. She could feel a yearning whose power surprised her, a hunger for the man beside her, for the feel of his arms around her, his lips, his strong body.

Once again, as in the kitchen earlier, she experienced a moment's disbelief that this could be happening to her. She'd been so careful about controlling her emotions and making sensible choices. How was it that suddenly she seemed to be spinning out of control? She drew a deep breath of gratitude for Chris's presence. If he wasn't here, if she and Ben had come alone, who could tell what might have happened? And yet a secret inner core of her wished that they *were* alone . . .

They paddled back lazily, and even though Chris kept insisting that he was fine and couldn't they paddle faster, Ben said, "We'll go out again tomorrow. No point using everything we got now." Jenny had seen Chris wince as he grasped the paddle, also the blisters forming and sunburn on the back of his neck, and she knew Ben was aware of the limits of twelve-year-old strength. She said nothing, letting them work it out between them.

"Are we going to fish with that popper thing tomorrow?" Chris asked as they pulled in close to their own dock.

"What's that?" Jenny asked.

Ben reached out to steady the canoe against the dock. "It's a fly the bass like. Just a piece of cork with some feathers poking out in back. We thought we might give it a try." He stepped out of the canoe and made the line fast, all in one graceful motion. Then he turned and put out both hands to Jenny, helping her onto the dock easily. Chris scrambled out after them.

"You know, we could try it right now if we wanted to," the boy said. "I mean, we might catch something for supper like we did before. How about it, Ben?"

Ben hesitated, looking at Jenny. "It's up to the lady of the house. Are you in the mood for another fish dinner in the company of two hungry fishermen?"

"Well, let me consider that for a minute," Jenny said with pretended seriousness. The three of them stood on the dock, sun-warmed and content in each other's company. And it was at that precise moment that Jenny became aware that they weren't alone. Her gaze swung to the sloping path that led to the house. A man was standing at the head of the path just in front of the pine woods, looking down at them.

Jenny's heart flipped over and then plummeted.

"Philip!" she exclaimed in a breathy voice.

She could feel a change in Ben, a sudden tension coming over him. Chris's reaction was more overt. "Aw, gee," he said, and there was audible disappointment in his voice.

Jenny did her best to rally. She stepped forward as the man came down the rest of the way to the dock. He was slender and fair-haired, with clear gray eyes and a ready smile. He was dressed in a yellow knit shirt, beige pants and loafers. There was an unmistakable look of the city about him.

"Jenny!" He enveloped her in a hug and kissed her.

"Philip, you should have told me you were coming," she said in an uncertain voice. She was intensely aware of Ben Sullivan standing behind her. Philip released her and took a step toward Chris, tousling the boy's hair affectionately.

"Hi there, Chris," he said heartily. Jenny saw her son flinch from his touch, and her uneasiness increased a notch.

"Philip Boyd," he said with a smile, holding his hand out to Ben. Ben took it at once and said evenly, "Ben Sullivan."

"Whatever made you decide to come all the way up here?" Jenny asked. "I mean, I didn't expect—"

"Hey, you've been gone three whole days. I missed you. That's reason enough, isn't it?" He kissed her again, and Jenny sensed that Ben was keeping his emotions carefully in check. She didn't look at him, unable to face the expression in his face.

"Well, let's all go up to the house," she said with false brightness, knowing she had to handle this situation somehow. "We've just had a wonderful paddle around the lake." She led the way, with Philip keeping hold of her hand.

A gray Saab was parked in the driveway.

"Drove up from Boston, Mr. Boyd?" Ben asked.

"Philip, please. Yes, decided to treat myself to a weekend in Maine. Have to start back Sunday morning."

"You're an attorney?"

"Yes. Jenny told you?"

"No." Ben's face remained serious as he eyed the smart little Saab, the unmussed casual clothes. "No, she didn't. Just a hunch."

"You vacationing here, Ben?" Philip's voice was friendly, but Jenny could detect an edge of curiosity.

"No. I'm one of the locals."

"Ben's been very helpful," Jenny said in a rush. "The place was quite a mess when we arrived. I don't know how we'd have managed without him." They were standing uncertainly in the drive. "Shall we go in?" she said.

"Thanks," Ben said. "I'll be getting on home now. Nice meeting you, Philip."

"Are we going fishing tomorrow, Ben?" Chris asked. "Are we going to try the popper?"

Ben put a hand on the boy's shoulder. "We'll see, Chris. That can always wait for another time."

Philip said quickly, "Hey, don't let me upset any of your plans. You two go right ahead with whatever you were going to do. Jenny and I have a lot to catch up on."

"We'll talk about it tomorrow, then," Ben said. Jenny watched as he climbed into his pickup in that swift fluid motion she'd come to know. Something inside her twisted painfully.

"Seems like a nice fellow," Philip said as the truck disappeared down the driveway and they turned to go inside. Chris made straight for his room and slammed the door behind him. In seconds the sound of the television could be heard.

"Yes. He's been very kind to Chris—teaching him to fish and so on." Jenny's voice sounded, to her own ears, stiff and artificial, but Philip didn't seem to notice.

"I suppose the local people know a lot about that sort of thing," he said casually. He stood in the middle of the main room and looked around. "So this is the famous Carmichael retreat. You know, invitations to this place are rare and highly prized in Boston legal circles."

"Yes, I'm sure." Jenny knew that Philip would dearly love to be honored with such an invitation.

"Your dad's kept it simple. Very classy. That's the kind of guy he is. From what I hear," he added pointedly. Then, turning to her, he said with a look of exasperated patience, "Honestly, Jenny, wouldn't it be nice if you finally made up with him?"

Jenny took a deep breath, determined not to be hard on Philip just because he clearly wanted to be able to address her father as Buzz. Philip was still a good man. Hardworking, unfailingly kind. And besides, she reminded herself, Philip was reality. He was the world she lived in. Ben was fire and excitement. He was a man who lived in the woods and knew how to fish and swing an ax, who watched ospreys and waited for a moose to come and drink at the water's edge. But he was from a world that Jenny was inhabiting for only a month. When that month was over, she'd be back in Boston, working alongside Philip at the law firm of Prescott, Turner and Bowing. She had struggled long and hard to become a lawyer. She was so near attaining it now; she mustn't let anything get in the way. She and Philip belonged together. When they were married...

"I think my father and I understand each other," she said, stopping the flow of her thoughts. "Maybe it's better if we keep out of each other's way."

"Well, I won't argue with you. I'm too happy just to be with you," he said, moving to take her in his arms again. "You've no idea how much I've missed you."

Jenny smiled at him. "I missed you, too, Philip," she said, and hoped heaven would forgive her for that lie.

After a moment he stepped back and said, "I'd better bring in my things."

Jenny felt herself grow rigid. "Oh, not here, Philip," she blurted.

She saw his puzzled look. "I mean, there's a wonderful guest house just through the trees there."

"Guest house?" Hurt was now added to puzzlement.

"Chris's room is right here, and it would be very unsuitable—awkward, that is."

"Oh, Jenny, really." His brows drew together with annoyance. Then, struggling, he said, "All right, whatever you say."

"I'll bring some clean sheets." She hurried off to look for them, breathing a sigh of relief.

Lying in bed that night, Jenny found images of the evening replaying through her head. Dinner, with Philip carrying most of the conversation, Chris getting up from the table when they were done and starting wordlessly for his room. She had called him back sharply.

"Chris! I think you've forgotten to say good-night."

"Oh. Good night."

Jenny wished she hadn't said anything. His grim compliance had only made things worse, and now all the anxieties about her son seemed to surface again. She could feel the tight little lines forming on her forehead. They had sat by the fire in the main room after dinner, she and Philip, with Philip looking so contented, so reliable, so *safe*. Safety certainly counted. For both herself and Chris. It was what they needed above all else. And yet... She turned restlessly in bed. Had she ever in her life felt safer than this afternoon, sliding over the lake in the fragile canoe, feeling the strong, steady strokes of Ben's paddle guiding them? What was safety, anyway, and how did you determine it?

She had pleaded tiredness, and Philip had left early, with a reluctant sigh, trudging along the path to the guest cottage, which Jenny had prepared for him. Now, still very much awake, she could hear the sound of distant thunder. Was the storm headed this way? She listened, trying to decide, and then heard something else. Music, far away and elusive, weaving its way through the quiet night woods. She listened for a long time before falling asleep.

CHAPTER FOUR

JENNY HELD her mug of coffee in both hands and looked over its rim to the dock, where Chris was practicing his fly casting. Sitting on the narrow porch in the morning mist, she watched as his arm came back again and again, slowly gaining skill and sureness, until the casts began to look fairly respectable and the line swept out cleanly in front of him. It must be Ben's rod he was using, she thought.

She squeezed her eyes shut for a moment, wondering why she should be attracted to someone as unsuitable as Ben Sullivan. All her ambitions, all her hard work, were centered in the city. Boston was where her future lay, her security. And Chris's. She had absolutely no business being distracted by dark blue eyes, thick black hair and a mobile mouth that could grin engagingly or press down on hers with a fire that started her blood surging. She opened her eyes and took a deep breath. She and Philip had been making plans for the better part of a year. They had interests in common, shared work and goals. They enjoyed each other's company in quiet ways. Wasn't that enough? Yes, Jenny told herself firmly. Of course it was.

Trying to shift the focus of her thoughts, she scanned the overcast sky and wondered if the clouds would lift or if it was going to turn into a rainy day.

"Hey, good morning." She heard the screen door slam as Philip came out.

She turned and waved her cup at him. "Coffee's right there on the counter. Help yourself."

She heard him pour it and then return. He was wearing jeans and a sweatshirt today. He leaned over to kiss her and then dropped into a slat-backed Adirondack chair beside her. His hair was slightly mussed.

"How'd you sleep?" she asked.

He breathed in deeply and said, "Very well. A little chilly and lonely, but I must confess I slept."

"Oh, but I put extra blankets out for you," she protested.

"No. Not that kind of chilly...."

Jenny said quickly, "I do hope it's not going to rain all day."

"Occasional showers, the radio said."

How like Philip, she thought, to have paid attention to that. "Well, there's plenty to do even so. Some wonderful little towns around here, and a few places I suspect have great antiques."

He sipped his coffee and motioned with his head toward Chris on the dock. "Don't tell me we're going to have to catch our breakfast."

"No, silly. He's just practicing his fly casting. Ben Sullivan's been teaching him." As she said Ben's name, she wondered if her feelings were written plainly on her face, but Philip said only, "Ben... Oh, that local fellow. Yes, I imagine there's quite a trick to it."

Not a trick at all, Jenny thought a bit resentfully. With Ben it was an art.

"I'll fix you some breakfast," she said with false cheer. "You just sit here and enjoy your coffee while I get it ready."

As she got to her feet, he said, "Of course I shouldn't mention business up here, but when you do come back to Boston we're going to have to get right to work on that Avery case."

"Yes, I know. I brought some of the papers up here with me. I thought I might have a chance to look it over." Actually she hadn't given it a thought. Not from the moment she'd arrived. "Would you like to see them?"

"I would," he said, his face brightening. "I could just run over some of the aspects of that trust that I've had on my mind."

"I'll get them for you," she said, turning away, but he stopped her.

"Don't bother. Just tell me where they are and I'll find them. You go ahead with breakfast."

"Right inside the door there," she said, pointing to her bedroom. "The briefcase is on the floor."

She went to the kitchen and began pulling out eggs, bacon, English muffins. Fat and cholesterol concerns would have to be put on hold for the time being, she decided. Country-breakfast smells began to fill the house, and she could hear Philip still rummaging about in the bedroom.

There was a sudden knock on the screen door, and Ben's voice called, "Hi there. Chris up yet?"

Jenny's heart pounded and color flared into her cheeks.

"Oh, good morning," she said, going to the door with a long cooking fork in one hand. "Yes. Didn't you see him down at the dock? Would you like some breakfast?"

Ben was wearing a navy blue turtleneck shirt tucked into his worn jeans. The morning mist had dampened his hair. There was no pickup in sight, so he must have walked over.

"Had mine already," he said curtly, avoiding her eyes. "I told Chris we'd go fishing today, although the weather looks a little uncertain. Still, it shouldn't really stop us...."

"Hi, Ben!" Chris came hurrying up the slope from the lake. "I've been practicing casting."

"Good for you."

"Well, come on in, both of you," Jenny said, holding the door open. "Chris, you'll want something to eat, I'm sure."

Before they could enter, Philip came out of the bedroom, papers in hand, and said, "That smells good." He saw the two at the door. "Well, good morning, Chris, Ben."

"Hi," Chris said without enthusiasm. Ben said good morning, but his expression was fixed and unsmiling.

Philip put the papers down and went to join them just outside the door, scanning the sky. "What do you think today'll be like?" he asked Ben. "You people up here probably read the signs better than the weathermen." Before Ben could speak, though, Philip continued, "Chris, it looks as if you're getting to be an expert with that rod." He put out a hand and clapped the boy on the shoulder. As he did so Blaze leapt on Philip, nearly knocking him off his feet. Ben quickly had the animal by the collar and pulled him away.

"Blaze, down!" he ordered. He turned to Philip. "Sorry. He's nervous about sudden movements. You all right?"

"Sure," Philip said, regaining his footing and brushing at the damp paw prints on his sweatshirt. "No harm done." But he eyed the dog warily.

Ben said to Jenny, "Is it all right if I take Chris out fishing today? That is, if there's no storm."

"Yes, of course." Jenny wished he would meet her gaze.

"Oh, boy!" Chris said, but Ben was already walking away with the two dogs at his heels. "Back later," he said over his shoulder to Chris. "Have yourself some breakfast."

After they'd finished eating and Chris had left them, Philip said, "I didn't want to mention this in front of him, but do you think it's wise to let Chris go out in a boat with that fellow? You hardly know him."

I know him well enough to trust him with my life. Or Chris's. "He seems very capable to me," she said, trying to sound reasonable.

"Well, it's just that it isn't a very promising day, and I imagine storms can come up without much warning."

"I'm sure Ben will take that into account."

"And I don't think that dog's safe for the boy to be around, either," Philip said. "Seems rather vicious and temperamental to me. You can't trust an animal like that."

Trust, Jenny thought. How could she explain to Philip, city-bred and city-wary, that sometimes you could trust someone without clear-cut reasons? Besides, it was his hand coming down on Chris's shoulder that had set the dog off. Maybe Blaze was just being protective?

"Please don't worry about it," she said. "My father's known Ben for years." It was not strictly the truth. She had no idea how long Buzz Carmichael had known him or indeed what he thought of him. But it seemed to be an argument that worked with Philip.

"Oh, okay, then, I suppose..." He trailed off, then downed the remainder of his coffee. He started to get up from the table. "Still," he said, "it reminds me of something else I've been wanting to speak to you about."

Jenny began gathering plates. "What's that?"

"Well, about Chris. It seems to me that what might straighten him out faster than anything would be a really good school. Someplace with a first-rate reputation. I thought after we're married..."

"Send him away, you mean?" Jenny turned to him, a plate in each hand.

"Uh, yes. The experience of living away from home and doing some concentrated studying in a controlled environment might do him a world of good."

Jenny struggled to keep her temper. For some reason it was the phrase *straighten him out* that rasped against her already raw nerves.

"I know you mean well, Philip," she said carefully. "And I know I've had some problems with Chris, but I don't think he really needs straightening out, as you put it. He may need something, and if he does, I'll help him find it, but I'm not sending him anywhere. He stays with me." She spun around quickly and placed the plates in the sink.

Philip was behind her at once, his hands on her shoulders.

"Jenny, dear, I'm sorry. I didn't mean to offend you. We'll work it out together. Of course we will. We're going to be a family."

He turned her around and kissed her gently. Philip was always gentle, she thought. Always caring, always there when she needed him. Why was it becoming so difficult for her to picture a life with him, picture the two of them—and Chris—together as a family?

The day proved to be only intermittently showery, and after Philip had spent the morning absorbed in the legal papers Jenny had brought with her, they were able to go out and explore some of the small towns in the region. Philip, with his interest in antiques and local architecture, seemed to enjoy himself.

When they returned late in the afternoon, Jenny went to the window that looked out over the lake. She could see a small boat near the point where they'd picnicked the day before. As soon as it started back, she cast a quick glance at Philip, absorbed now in the Portland newspaper he'd bought, and said, "I'll just be out for a minute, Philip."

She hurried down to the dock and waited for the little motorboat to come in.

"Hey, Mom, wait'll you see the fish we caught!" Chris said as they pulled up to the dock. Ben put the cooler chest on the dock and vaulted after it in one graceful motion. "We're gonna cook 'em at Ben's house," Chris went on, climbing out after him.

"Was that a question?" Ben asked.

"Oh. I mean, is it okay if we cook 'em at Ben's?"

"Yes, of course, if Ben doesn't mind." His nearness was making her pulses race. She longed to reach out and touch him, to feel the hair that had curled unexpectedly in the dampness.

"Did you enjoy the day?" he asked, looking at her for the first time. The look carried irony and a polite but impersonal quality that was somehow painful.

"Oh, yes. We saw something of the countryside, did a little exploring." She was doing her best to sound normal.

One black eyebrow shot up. "Really. I'd have thought indoor pursuits would have been more suitable for a day like this."

Jenny stared at him as realization dawned on her. The scene that morning, with Ben at the kitchen door and Philip emerging from her bedroom. Ben must have thought... She tried to put words together, but her throat was too dry for speech.

Ben went on, "There's plenty of fish. You and Philip are welcome to come along and share if you like."

Because he doesn't care, Jenny thought painfully. He was throwing out a casual invitation as a way of letting her know how little it matters to him. But being with Philip and looking across the table at Ben would be torture for her. "No, I think Philip and I will go out for dinner," she said. "I'm sure he'll want a Maine lobster before he goes back."

"Ah, yes, a lobster." Ben smiled, a one-sided smile that made Jenny long to put a finger at the corner of his mouth where a small indentation appeared. "Just what all the city folks want when they come here." He turned to Chris. "All set, partner? Let's start cleaning these fish."

"Okay. See you later, Mom."

"Oh, will you mind if I leave my boat here for a while?" Ben asked. "I usually keep it down at Ross McIntyre's place."

"No, of course not."

Jenny watched them go up the slope, Ben in the lead with the cooler balanced on one shoulder, the tackle box in his hand, Chris following with the rods. Jenny's eyes followed the tall figure with its easy, masculine stride until he disappeared into the trees.

When she returned to the house, she found Philip dozing in the chair by the window with the newspaper in his lap. For a moment she just stood looking at him, conflicting emotions warring inside her. She desperately tried to put the pieces of her life back into the pattern she had made for herself, the plan that had gone shattering in every direction the day Ben had pulled her against him and kissed her. Philip was certainty, reliability. Above all, he was reality. He would fit into her life. With Philip she would never have to worry about being alone. She would always have someone to turn to. As she kept cataloging the arguments, lining them up on an invisible scoreboard, she reminded herself that love wasn't everything. She'd tried that once and it hadn't worked. But that had been nothing but teenage foolishness, not the thundering emotion Ben Sullivan drew from her.

She looked again at the man in the chair, so vulnerable in sleep. Anyway, she *did* love Philip. There were all kinds of love, that was all. And what she felt for him was the kind of love you could build a life on. That was important, wasn't it?

He stirred, awoke, looked up at her. "There you are," he said lazily. "I'm afraid all the fresh air got to me. But I've had a good idea. Why don't we go out for dinner? Find ourselves a couple of those famous Maine lobsters."

Jenny swallowed. "Yes. Of course. Good idea, Philip."

THE SAAB PULLED out of the drive shortly after noon the next day, with Jenny and Chris standing in the doorway waving Philip off. Jenny had insisted Chris be present, and he went through the motions, although with little enthusiasm.

"You guys should've eaten with us last night," he told her when they went back inside. "That fish was something the way Ben cooked it."

"I'm sure it was." Jenny longed to ask about Ben, whether he would be coming by today, what they'd talked about, but she held back, determined not to give it too much importance. Earlier, she'd glanced down at the dock and seen that the little motorboat was gone.

She looked at her son. "You've had a good time with Ben, haven't you?"

"Yeah. He knows a lot of neat stuff."

"I'm glad. You'll have all those neat things to remember when we go back to Boston." She crossed to the sink and began running water over the lunch dishes. When Chris didn't answer, she turned to find him scowling at the floor, his hands in the pockets of his jeans. She turned off the water. "Chris?"

"I wish we didn't have to go back," he said.

Jenny was determined not to take *that* seriously. "But we have to, though. And just think of all the things you'll have learned to do this summer. Canoeing and fishing and how to tie flies and—"

"You can't do any of that stuff back home."

She could feel irritability stealing in. "Well, we'll just be grateful we've been lucky enough to have had such a good vacation. And who knows? Maybe we'll be able to do it again."

His expression became dark and sullen. "You're going to marry Philip, aren't you?"

The words, flung out angrily, lay between them, an impassable barrier.

"Philip loves us," Jenny said, trying to sound firm and positive. "He wants us to be together, to be a family. He wants to take care of us. Anyway, that's a decision for me to make, not you."

"Well, I don't want him to take care of me!" Chris exploded. "And I don't want us to be a family, either!" Chin firmly set, he marched out of the kitchen and into his bedroom, slamming the door behind him. Jenny let her breath out slowly, realizing that every muscle in her body was painfully taut. She went back to the sink and plunged her hands into the hot water, trying to keep anger under control.

She straightened the house, gathered up damp towels, dusted, picked up a book and read for a time. But it didn't hold her interest, so she put it aside, walked down to the dock and watched the family of mergansers paddle by. All the time her ears were alert, listening for the sound of Ben's pickup or the clamor of the dogs at his heels. But the woods and the lake were silent, and presently the sun disappeared behind a cloud. A heavy darkness moved in. Rain was on the way again.

She went back up to the house and started thinking about what to fix for dinner. Maybe now was a good time for the frozen pizzas she'd bought earlier. Not that Chris deserved them, she thought crossly.

He ate the pizza, but without enthusiasm or conversation. Then he bolted back into his room, and she heard the TV come on. She sighed and made herself a cup of tea. She carried it into the living room and plopped down on the couch. She could hear the tapping of rain just starting up, bringing a chill with it, and got up to close the big windows that faced the lake. When she returned to the couch, she saw the papers

Philip had been studying. She picked them up and began to read through them, trying to make sense of legal matters that had been quite clear to her in Boston, but that now were elusive and obscure. She put them down, lifted her feet up on the couch and lay back, listening to the rain.

She woke with a start, feeling frozen. The room was dark and the rain was coming down harder. She should have started a fire. Shivering, she got up and managed to turn on a light, but then as she hugged herself for warmth, she became aware of the cabin's stillness. She hurried to Chris's door and flung it open. The room was dark and empty. Fear rose in her throat. She hurried to the kitchen, turning on lights as she went.

"Chris?" She went to the back door and looked out. Her car was gone.

Stumbling, she hurried back into the living room and seized the telephone, fumbling as she sought the scrap of paper on which she'd written Ben's number.

"Ben? It's Jenny. Is Chris with you?"

"No." His voice was instantly alert. "When did he go out?"

"I don't know. I fell asleep. When I woke up he wasn't here. And...my car's gone."

"I'll be right over."

She was waiting for him, in a hooded poncho, when his pickup came roaring through the rain moments later. Barely stopping, he opened the door on the passenger side and waited for her to climb in, then turned around in the wide place in front of the house and drove off, this time heading for the county road. His hands gripped the wheel tightly, and his mouth was set in a grim line. He, too, was wearing a poncho, its hood tossed back.

"It'll be all right, Jenny," he said. "He can't have gone far."

But he could have, Jenny thought. He could be on the turnpike this minute, headed who knows where. Ben seemed to be reading her thoughts.

"Even if he made it to the turnpike, the highway patrol would pick him up quickly. He's just a kid."

"You said yourself he looks older."

"Older, but not old enough to fool a cop. Anyway, we'll probably catch up with him before he gets that far. We'll find him." He paused, squinting into the rain as they reached the county road. He swung the pickup to the right. "He's a little young to know how to drive, isn't he?"

Jenny let her breath out in an agonized sigh. "He's gotten in with older boys in Boston. I guess he's learned." She paused, then went on in a low monotone, "It's my fault. I was always working or in class—"

"Don't blame yourself for everything, Jenny."

She hurried on, ignoring the interruption. "But I should tell you, this kind of thing's happened before. I mean, he's gotten into scrapes. One of them involved a car."

"Stolen?"

"Yes, I'm afraid so. He wasn't driving, but he was there. They let him off because of his age." Her voice broke, and she burst out, "Ben, what am I going to do?"

He didn't answer the question, but asked, "Was there something that brought this about? Did you have some kind of quarrel?"

Jenny heard again her son's angry outburst. *I don't want him to take care of me! And I don't want us to be a family, either!*

"Uh, yes, we did. Chris was upset about the idea of returning to Boston after our holiday. He'd like to...to stay here. He doesn't understand why that's impossible." She avoided any mention of Philip.

"I see."

"He's had such a good time with you, learning about fishing and all those other things. I suppose he doesn't want it to end."

"I'm sorry. Perhaps I shouldn't have—"

"No. Don't say that. It's been wonderful for him. I just don't know what I'm going to do, that's all. But it's my problem, not yours."

This time Ben didn't answer, but kept his eyes on the road, leaning forward to peer through the rain-streaked windshield.

"I'm just praying he hasn't been gone long," she breathed. "Then there might be a chance of finding him."

"We'll find him," he said firmly.

Moments later Jenny felt fear leap into her throat as she saw a revolving blue light at the side of the road. A police car had pulled up next to another vehicle, which Jenny recognized as her own compact, skewed at an oblique angle and sitting in the midst of what looked like a pile of splintered lumber.

"Oh, Ben!" she cried, grabbing for the door handle.

His strong hand reached for her, pulling her back. "He's all right. He's there."

And then she saw Chris, standing huddled and wet beside an officer, the two figures in the beam of Ben's headlights. The boy was in his sweatshirt and jeans, both soaked through.

"Oh, thank God," Jenny said, and leaned forward, her head resting for a moment in both her hands. When, she sat up and reached for the door again, Ben stopped her.

"Stay here. Let me handle this."

He was out of the truck before she could protest, and she watched as he strode over to the officer and began to speak to him. In the eerie blue light she could see the rain streaking down his poncho and running off his hair. He put out one hand and rested it on Chris's shoulder, but didn't look at the boy while he talked earnestly to the man. Jenny saw the officer nod, rain dripping off the plastic cover of his uniform hat.

Then Ben walked with Chris back to the truck and opened the door on Jenny's side. "There's a blanket in the back there. Can you reach it?" he asked.

Jenny scrambled for it and handed it to him. He wrapped it around Chris and helped him into the truck, then went around to the driver's side and climbed in.

"Are you all right?" Jenny asked her son, but there was an ominous chill in her voice. She could feel her immense relief draining away, being replaced by anger.

He nodded without speaking.

"What did you think you were doing, anyway?" she demanded. "Where were you going?"

His thin shoulders lifted in a shrug.

"I should have realized you weren't to be trusted," she said in a voice that was unsteady with fury. "After what happened in Boston, I don't know what made me think you'd behave any differently up here. Apparently we'll have to come up with a new set of rules."

Ben said calmly, "It looks as if your car isn't seriously damaged, in spite of that mess of lumber. Chris here skidded on the wet road and went headfirst into Mr. Hopworth's vegetable stand. You have a few fairly sizable dents, though. Officer Berton's calling a tow truck. We'll see about that tomorrow after you both appear in court."

Jenny spun around to face him. "Court!"

He turned the key in the ignition and swung the pickup out into the road again, making a careful turn and heading back the way they'd come. "I'm afraid so."

"But he's only twelve!" she cried. "He's a juvenile."

Ben replied calmly, "Yes, I explained that to the officer. But around here juveniles still have to answer for what they do, and so do their parents."

"It was my own car!" Jenny protested.

"True. But it was Mr. Hopworth's vegetable stand."

With a groan, Jenny leaned her head back against the seat and said no more as they drove home through the rain. Once or twice she stole a look at Ben's profile, rugged and serious as it had been the first day they'd met, all traces of intimacy, even of friendship, erased. But she could no longer think about him or what might have been between them. Now all her thoughts were dark despairing ones centered on her son and how she should cope with this latest crisis. She had a strong feeling that what Chris needed more than anything was a steady masculine influence. He'd taken to Ben Sullivan and wanted to learn all Ben had to teach. But one month in a fleeting summer didn't solve a problem as big as Chris's. For perhaps the first time,

Jenny faced the unpleasant truth that it was a problem, and a major one.

She glanced at her son in the dim light of the truck and saw that his young features were pinched and resentful. Everything seemed spoiled, all the earlier magic gone. Ben turned left onto the dirt road that led to the lake houses, and she felt the truck slide in the mud. He adjusted the wheel slightly and shifted down. The truck righted itself and plowed ahead. He was a stranger again, Jenny thought. That afternoon by the lake might never have been. It was all blotted out. And it wasn't only this business of Chris that had done it. It was Philip's visit. She had sensed it the very first moment on the dock when Philip had strolled down and kissed her in that proprietary way. Something had changed then, some tension had sprung up altering the very air around them. And yesterday morning, when he'd come to the door and seen Philip coming out of her bedroom...

They pulled up in front of the house and almost at once Chris reached for the door handle and let himself out of the truck, leaving the soggy blanket behind. He dashed for the house and disappeared inside without a word. Jenny raised a hand to her forehead in a gesture of weariness.

"I'm really grateful to you for your help," she said to Ben, but the words came out sounding like something formal and memorized.

His hand shot out as she prepared to leave the pickup, closing around her wrist and holding her there.

"Jenny, don't worry about this. It'll be all right."

Would anything ever be right in her life again? Jenny could only nod numbly and wish with all her heart that Ben would put his arms around her and hold her tight against him. But the hand on her wrist was firm and authoritative, not loving and comforting. It was an order for her to get hold of herself.

"Don't give up on Chris," he said, and the words sounded almost harsh.

"I'd never do that," she whispered. "Even though I feel like throttling him right now."

"Okay, get some sleep. And be in court at nine in the morning." He paused. "Wait. You don't have a way to get there. Perhaps I could—"

"No, please. Don't bother," she said suddenly. "We've troubled you enough. I'll find a ride. I'm sure there's at least one taxi in town." She couldn't tell him that it was painful for her to be close enough to touch him and yet fear his rejection.

"If you say so," he said quietly, and then for a moment he was silent. She could feel his gaze on her. Rain streaked down the windshield and beat on the roof of the pickup. The strong hand that held her wrist relaxed its hold and withdrew. He faced front and she could see his profile again, craggy and unforgiving.

She pushed the door open and climbed down, not bothering to pull up her hood, not caring about the rain that soaked her.

CHAPTER FIVE

SHE WAS on the telephone early the next morning. "You mean there's no driver available?"

"Well, not at the moment, no. When Fred comes in, I'll tell him you need a ride."

"When will that be?"

The voice at the other end sounded unconcerned. "Oh, he generally comes in around ten or so in the summer. Winters, of course, he drives the school—"

"Is there any other taxi in town?"

"None as I know of."

"Thank you." Jenny put down the receiver crossly and paced across the room, putting her hands at the sides of her head where she could feel an anxious throbbing.

Chris opened the door of his bedroom and came out, wearing clean jeans and a neat denim shirt. Jenny flicked an impatient glance at him, and Philip's arguments in favor of a stern private school leapt to her mind.

"Have we got a ride?" Chris asked in a subdued voice.

"Not so far, but I'll think of something," she said. And then, "Chris, before we go, there's something I want to say. You're my son, and I...I love you no matter what." Her voice faltered slightly, but she made it firm again and went on, "But this kind of behavior is unacceptable. It's worse than that. It's criminal, and I'm sure you know that. If it happens again, we'll return to Boston immediately. And once we get there—"

She was interrupted by the sound of a car coming up the drive. She went to the back door and saw Adele Hazelton's old Plymouth. Still shaky with anger, Jenny managed a wave, which Adele returned cheerily.

"Heard you might be needing a ride into town," she called out. "You about ready?"

Jenny took a deep breath to steady herself. "Oh, Adele, you're a lifesaver. Thank you so much." She turned back to Chris and said tersely, "Let's go."

"Ben gave me a call," Adele said in a low voice when Jenny reached her. Chris was trailing far behind. "Now don't you go worrying about it. It'll be all right. These things happen."

Jenny felt color flooding her cheeks. "I know. Ben's been very kind. I don't know what I'd have done last night if he hadn't helped us."

Adele was dressed today in a flowered cotton dress with a pink sweater over it. She patted Jenny's hand where it rested on the car door. "My sister's boy got in trouble more times than you could shake a stick at," she whispered. "Ben helped them out, too. He's like that." She broke off as Chris approached.

"Well, hi there," Adele said. "You must be Chris. All right, you two, climb in."

"Mrs. Hazelton's kindly offered us a ride," Jenny said. Her anger was dying down and now, seeing her son more as a scared boy than a cocky delinquent, she softened slightly.

"I was going into town, anyway," Adele explained, as they went clanking and wheezing back down the wooded drive toward the county road. "Looks like it's making out for a good day after all the rain, doesn't it?''

During the ride into town she kept up a friendly chatter. "Highbush blueberries are looking real good this year. They'll be ripe before you go back to the city. Staying out the month, aren't you? Last week in July they ought to be just prime. You come over to my back field, bring a couple of buckets, and you can pick all you want. I'll let you know as soon as they're ready."

"Thank you," Jenny said, trying to sound enthusiastic. "That ought to be fun. Right, Chris?" There was no answer from the back seat, but Adele seemed unconcerned.

"Well, now, here we are," she said, pulling up in front of a small one-story frame building next door to the post office. It had a humble look, as if it might have served as a general store in other times but had been revamped to accommodate village offices. Jenny saw a small sign in the window: Tax Collector, Municipal Court.

"We take the door on the left," Adele explained, leading the way.

"Thank you again, Adele. We really appreciate it. We can find the way now, I'm sure."

"Oh, that's all right, I'm going there, too," Adele said matter-of-factly. "I'm the court clerk."

Jenny paused for a moment to give her a surprised look, then proceeded into a room that was simply furnished with rows of wooden chairs. There was a heavy oak table at the front and a smaller table to one side of it.

"There won't be anybody here but you," Adele whispered to Jenny. "When it's a juvenile, nobody else is allowed in. The judge hears other cases separately."

Jenny nodded, not feeling particularly reassured, and watched as Adele took her place at the smaller table and began sorting papers briskly. The room still held a morning chill, and Jenny, dressed in a beige skirt and navy blazer—the only suitable outfit she'd brought—shivered slightly and stole a look at her watch. One minute before nine.

"I don't know what's going to happen here," she said to Chris in a flat voice, "but I just hope you know how to conduct yourself—"

A door at the side opened and she heard Adele say, "Good morning, Judge Sullivan."

Jenny's eyes flew to the tall figure who'd entered the room. Her blood, which had felt cold and congealed, suddenly turned hot, flushing her face with color. Ben paused to murmur something to Adele, then took his place at the big oak table. He was dressed in his usual plaid shirt, except that this morning he'd added a tie and exchanged his jeans for a pair of neat beige trousers.

"Good morning," he said, his glance taking in both her and Chris. His voice was impersonal, and no smile went with it. "Won't you sit down? Right there will be fine." He indicated the first row of chairs.

Jenny sat and pulled an obviously bewildered Chris down next to her. She wanted to say something, but no words came as she watched Ben put on a pair of horn-rimmed glasses and calmly pick up an official-looking report. Something about the dignity of the court—even in such an unlikely place as Tucker's Pond—prevented her from speaking. But her thoughts were spinning. How could he have deceived her this way? Not telling her who he really was, making her think . . . For the first time she glanced at Chris and saw that he, too,

was flushed. What would this do to him? He'd begun
to idolize Ben. How could he ever face him after this?

"I've reviewed Officer Berton's report of this case,"
he said at last, "and it seems to me there are two parts
to consider." He took off the reading glasses and went
on soberly, "There is, first of all, the matter of the
stolen car."

Jenny found her voice at last. "It's *my* car," she
said. "And I'm certainly not pressing charges."

"So noted," he said, not looking at her and ad-
dressing Chris. "Along with that, there is the matter of
driving without a license and jeopardizing public
safety. You could have easily hit a person or another
car, young man. *And* there is also Mr. Hopworth's
roadside stand, which you virtually demolished."

Jenny, glancing at Chris, saw his lower lip tremble
slightly.

"I'll pay for the damage to the stand," she said
quickly.

He looked at her sternly. "You're not the one who
destroyed it, Mrs. Carver. And I was speaking to
Chris."

Jenny bit her lip and was silent.

"All these factors make up a case serious enough to
deserve the court's attention," he went on. "Even
though the owner of the car is pressing no charges, and
even though I have spoken personally to Mr. Hopworth and assured him his loss will be covered. However, as I see it, they represent only one-half of the
problem."

Jenny started to speak again, caught his warning
look, and subsided.

"The other half is what led you to do it," he said to Chris. "And that is the half I consider more important." He paused briefly, then, "Why did you do it?"

Chris gave a shrug, then started to speak. Ben held up a hand. "No, I'm not looking for quick excuses. I don't want you to try to explain it to me. You're the one who needs to know the answer." He sat forward in his chair, hands clasped in front of him.

"We're all responsible for our own behavior, Chris. Things around you—people—may not always be to your liking, but you can't change them. There's no one you can change but yourself. And that's as true in Boston as it is in Tucker's Pond. Are you able to understand that?"

Chris nodded faintly and murmured, "Yes, sir."

"When a real problem comes up, it has to be faced," Ben went on quietly. "I want you to try doing that. I want you to take some time by yourself and think about it. Ask yourself if you're really facing your problems or just running away from them." He paused again. "That's what it all comes down to in the end, no matter how many people you talk to. It all comes down to you." He was looking sternly at Chris, but the look was not unkind. In the silence of the chilly little courtroom Jenny held her breath. He was right, so very right. How had she let her relationship with her son get so out of control?

"May we go now, Judge Sullivan?" she asked in a small voice, getting to her feet.

His expression became harsh again. "Laws have been broken here, Mrs. Carver. Please sit down."

Jenny sank back into the chair. "But he's only—"

"I realize Chris is only twelve. Even so, he will have to make restitution. Chris, will you stand up, please?"

The boy rose, and Jenny could sense, rather than see, the trembling of his thin frame. Her heart ached for him.

"First of all, you are to write a note to Mr. Hopworth, apologizing for wrecking his roadside stand. The clerk of the court will furnish you with his address. Understood?"

"Yes, sir." Chris's words were almost inaudible.

"Then you are to rebuild the stand."

"I already said I would pay for that," Jenny put in desperately. "If you'll give me the name of a local carpenter, I'll have it taken care of." Heaven only knew where *that* money would come from. But she would manage somehow.

His dark blue eyes turned to her again, cold as a winter pond. "I don't think you understood the sentence, Mrs. Carver. Chris is to rebuild it."

Jenny stared at him. Beside her, Chris said in a quavery voice, "I don't know how."

Ben gave him a direct, unrelenting look. "Then you'll have to learn, won't you?"

Despair washed over Jenny in a cold flood as she struggled to her feet once more. She could scarcely remember how they got out of the courtroom, except that Adele waylaid them at the door to whisper that Jenny's car was down the street at Bulmer's body shop and in good enough shape to drive home. Bulmer would give her an estimate on the dents, if she wanted one. "And don't worry yourself sick now. It's going to be all right."

Jenny could only nod and thank her, fighting back tears of total frustration. Holding tight to Chris's hand, she dragged him off down the street without a backward look at Ben Sullivan. What would happen

next? How could Chris possibly do something so obviously beyond his capabilities? And why, why, *why*
had she ever thought a vacation in Maine would help
either of them? Anger at her son mingled with a pro-
found sense of failure.

She listened with only half an ear to the explanations of Mr. Bulmer, a slow-speaking man with a greasy
shirt and an imposing stomach.

"Now she won't give you any trouble if you want to
drive her as is," he explained. "Tire blew, and I fixed
that right off. But you'll want to get them dents
straightened out and repainted before she rusts."

Jenny nodded impatiently and cut him short by asking for his bill. She wrote him a check and in order to
stop his stream of explanations said that he could send
her the estimate for the bodywork. Then she and Chris
drove home in rigid silence. Only when she stopped the
car in front of the house did she find her voice enough
to say, "I have no idea how all this is going to come
out, Chris. I just hope before you do something this
stupid again, you'll stop and consider the possibility
that you might not get off so easily next time." She
could feel the rigid, unforgiving set of her jaw.

He didn't answer, but got out of the car and made
his way down to the dock. As she headed for the
kitchen door she saw him standing staring out over the
water, his hands stiffly at his sides. How many times
had she hoped things would work out? And had they
ever?

Later when she called him in for lunch, neither of
them could find anything to say to each other. He ate
his sandwich, gulped his milk and then went into his
room, banging the door behind him. Jenny leaned

forward, her head in her hands, elbows resting on the table.

The old house's venerable kitchen stove had probably never in all its years of existence received the cleaning Jenny gave it that afternoon. While its burners were soaking in the sink, every surface was sprayed, scrubbed and polished to a burnished gleam. When that was done, she started in on the refrigerator, removing all its contents and every shelf to do the job completely. When she was satisfied that it was as clean as soap and water could make it, she got down on her hands and knees and scrubbed the worn linoleum, working at a furious, punishing pace, her anger finding its way into every swish and swirl of her soapy sponge.

She got to her feet late in the afternoon, exhausted, dumped the bucket outside the back door and went into the bathroom to take a long hot soak in the tub. She washed her hair and dried it, put on clean jeans and her Celtics sweatshirt and came back out to the kitchen. Sparkling surfaces shone back at her, testimony to her afternoon's work. She walked over to the sink, looked out the window at the late-afternoon sunlight slanting through the pines and drew a deep breath. It hadn't helped, she reflected glumly. She was every bit as frustrated as she'd been that morning. And it was a frustration that was growing.

She threw together a quick dinner and called Chris out of his room. He had a preoccupied look, as though his mind was elsewhere, and once again they ate in silence. When they were done, it was Chris who cleared the table and washed the dishes. His penitence touched her, slightly dissolving the hard knot of anger inside her.

"I'm going out for a little while," she said suddenly. "I won't be long."

"That's okay," he said. "I'm doing something."

She shot him a look. "I can trust you to stay here?"

"Yeah, Mom. You don't have to worry."

"All right. Back soon."

She walked along the road through the early evening with its lingering sunlight and long shadows, and even before she reached Ben's house she could hear music coming out through the open window. Mozart, she thought irrelevantly. Then after hesitating for a second, she marched up onto the porch and banged on the door.

He was wearing the horn-rimmed glasses and carrying a book when he answered her knock. She saw that one long brown finger marked his place. He had on the same plaid shirt as this morning, but he'd removed the tie.

"Well, hello, Jenny," he said mildly.

"I hope I'm not disturbing you, *Judge* Sullivan," she said coolly. "I thought there were some loose ends we didn't tie up in court today."

"Please, come in," he said, and without waiting for her to answer, led the way into the living room. He went to the stereo and turned down the volume until the music was only a soft background sound. Then he set his book and glasses on the coffee table and bent to put a match to a fire that had been newly laid in the fireplace. When the flames began to crackle around the kindling he stood up again and put one elbow on the rough wood mantel.

"Okay, shoot," he said pleasantly.

Jenny drew a deep breath. "I know what Chris did was wrong. I'm still furious with him. But what made you deceive me—us—that way? Pretending you were only a handyman when all the time you were a judge!" In spite of herself, she found herself staring at his dark eyes, which reflected sparks from the fire. Colors from the flames played along his jawline and caught in the small indentation in his chin.

"Oh, now, wait a minute. That sounds like a put-down—'only a handyman,'" he mimicked. "Actually a handyman is someone with a thousand skills."

"You know what I mean," she said.

"Besides, what difference does it make?"

"I felt like an absolute fool."

"You mean you'd have treated me differently if you'd known?"

"I mean just what I said. You deceived me. You weren't honest."

He hesitated a moment, then said, "The law is only a part of my life, Jenny. It's what I do, yes, but still, it's only a part. And if Chris hadn't run off with your car last night, you might have gone back to Boston without ever knowing. It would still have been the same me." His mouth turned up in a small smile. "And I didn't deceive you entirely. I did promise Jack Preston I'd help get the summer places in shape. Around here we help each other out that way."

Jenny paced the floor a moment, conscious of his gaze on her.

"And that court appearance this morning. That was all put on for our benefit, wasn't it? You're on vacation—you told me so."

He tipped his head slightly. "Well, yes, it's true I wasn't hearing any other cases today. We pretty much close down in July, except for the occasional unexpected crisis. Summer people whooping it up on a Saturday night—something like that."

"I know Chris needed it, but did you really do it just for his benefit?"

His eyebrows rose. "I'd have thought that was obvious."

"Obvious to anyone who didn't know..." Her voice trailed off.

"Didn't know what?" His black brows formed a frown.

"That you were getting even with me, too!" she burst out. "Because of Philip's being here. You were taking it out on me because you thought that I...that you and I..."

He took his elbow off the mantel and turned away from the fire, looking directly at her with an expression so dark that for a moment Jenny quailed inwardly.

"Is that what you think of me?" His voice was deep and rang with anger. "You think I'd do that to a kid over some personal peeve?" For a moment the two of them faced each other across the cheerful room, which was now thick with resentment. And suddenly Jenny knew that she had gone too far, said too much.

"No," she admitted. "I don't think that. I shouldn't have said it. It's just that I thought everything would be better once we were in Maine, and instead, everything's gone wrong from the start."

"Surely not everything," he said quietly.

She shot him a glance. His thunderous expression was dissolving slowly.

"But Chris is only twelve," she protested wearily. "And he admires you so much. What's this heavy-handed judicial approach going to do to him? He can never measure up to what you expect of him. You've set him an impossible task, and that's going to push his self-esteem right into the ground! He doesn't know how to rebuild that man's stand. Who's going to show him how?''

"I am."

"And furthermore, I'm not even sure you have the authority to deal this way in court with a juvenile. You've taken on—'' She stopped short. "What did you say?''

"I said, I am." One corner of his mouth tilted slightly upward. "If you hadn't run out of the courtroom so fast this morning I'd have told you. You can tell Chris I'll pick him up at seven-thirty tomorrow morning. We want to get to the lumberyard early.''

"You mean you're going to..."

"I've just said so, haven't I?''

Jenny felt indignation flowing away from her like air from a spent balloon. His eyes were still on her, their depths reflecting a mixture of tenderness and exasperation. Stunned into silence, she watched as he slowly crossed the room and stood before her, then pulled her to him. Jenny let herself lean against the reservoir of strength she could feel in him. Almost without her willing it, her head pressed against his shoulder, and the tight, angry muscles in her own body began to relax as small insistent flames began to lick up and down her spine, invading every part of her and making her shudder slightly.

"Jenny, Jenny. Things are going to work out," he said softly. "Don't try to take on the whole world by yourself." For a moment he just held her, then with one hand he tipped her face up to his and kissed her softly. She strained toward him, wanting more, wanting him.

He drew back, his hand moving to her hair, running through it. She could feel his breath riffling the strands. Then she lifted her face to him again, and his mouth descended again, enveloping hers, his tongue flicking lightly inside.

Her hands came up to circle his neck, to touch his hair, with fingers that had longed to touch it since the first day she'd seen him. She clung to him, holding his lips with her own, wanting to drown herself in the kiss. Then suddenly, as if someone had whispered a warning to her, she realized what she was doing and drew away.

"I have to go," she gasped. "I've left Chris alone. I mean, it's getting late." She pulled herself out of his arms and started to back toward the door. "Thank you for...explaining things to me. I'll tell Chris."

He stood watching her with a curious unreadable look. Behind him the fire, growing in strength, curled around the logs and sent sparks up the chimney. Jenny made a dive for the front door and hurried out into the soft lavender twilight.

She could hear a loon crying from the lake as she strode along the dirt road. A solitary, lonesome sound, she thought, yet she loved it. It had always meant Maine to her. Only tonight it struck her with particular poignancy, echoing deep inside her and setting her own feelings resonating.

Why had she responded so wildly to Ben's kiss? How was it that she had never felt such a surge of emotion when Philip kissed her? Philip represented everything she wanted in life. He was quiet and stable and attentive. But he had never set her on fire the way Ben had tonight. She appreciated Philip, she thought, biting her lower lip thoughtfully and tasting as she did so some faint clinging essence of Ben's kiss. Appreciated him, but was never really swept away by him. Something in Philip's attitude always seemed to suggest that, with him, lovemaking fitted into a schedule and that it would be followed by other matters of equal importance.

But what did she know about Ben Sullivan, after all? Jenny's toe caught on a stone in the shadowy road, making her stumble. For a moment she stopped, then continued walking more slowly. She knew almost nothing about him except that he loved the woods and the lake, that he knew where the osprey's nest was and where the old moose came to drink in the early evening. And he *had* deceived her, no matter what he said. But did that change anything? *You mean you'd have treated me differently if you'd known?* She could hear his voice with its forthright question, and at heart she knew the answer. Nothing would have made any difference. Only how could she even think of altering the life plan she'd made so painstakingly? So many years of struggle had gone into it, so many years of grinding apprenticeship at the law firm where she now had a foothold—or would have as soon as she finished her studies and passed the bar examinations. And Philip represented the very best kind of stability—a home for her and for Chris. And she *did* love him. She really did.

She rounded the curve in the road and came in sight of the house. Her compact car was still parked in front. Dented, but at least it was there. A light was on in Chris's room.

She pushed open the screen door and went into the kitchen. The evening was growing chilly. She closed the wooden door, as well, and went into the living room, turning on lights along the way. She looked for matches on the mantel and was just lighting a fire when Chris came out of his room. He held a paper in his hand and gave her a sidelong glance as if assessing her mood.

"I've been working on my letter," he said. His hair was mussed and sticking up in several places, as if fingers had been run through it.

"Your letter?"

"To Mr. Hopworth. Ben...uh, the judge said I had to write one."

"Oh, yes."

"Do you want to read it?"

"If you want me to."

He held it out to her. It was considerably smudged from erasures.

"I'll copy it in ink. I wanted to show it to you first. See if it's okay."

Jenny sat in a chair near a lamp and read:

Dear Mr. Hopworth,

You don't know me, but I'm the one who ran into your vegetable stand the other night and busted it up. My name is Christopher Carver, and I am twelve. I live in Boston. Judge Sullivan said I should write you and apologize, and he also said I'm supposed to rebuild your stand. I don't know how to do that yet, but I'm going to try. And I do apologize. I'm very sorry for what I did.

Yours truly,
Chris Carver

Scarcely trusting herself to speak, Jenny handed the letter back to him and gave him a quick hug, ignoring his less than perfect spelling.

"I don't think you could have put it any better," she said, doing her best to keep her voice under control, to stay casual and not make too much of it. "Go ahead and copy it and we'll mail it first thing tomorrow. Then perhaps you should get to bed. Ben Sullivan's coming to pick you up at seven-thirty."

"He is?" Sudden hope was followed by a darkening of the boy's features. "How come?"

"He's going to show you how to rebuild that stand. And I think perhaps he's going to work with you on it."

His apprehension seemed to deepen, his face closing down as it had done so many times in the past. His eyes slanted away from her, and he went back to his room without another word. Jenny could only try to imagine the anxieties that were warring within him. The tight knot that had loosened and miraculously dissolved when she was at Ben's house returned, lodging somewhere in the pit of her stomach. She crossed her arms over her midsection and sank onto the old couch, staring into the flames. Her thoughts were a furious jumble of worries—Chris, expensive dents to be repaired, that painfully wrought letter. *I don't know how I'm going to do that yet, but I'm going to try.* And pushing everything else to one side, the memory of those blue eyes just above hers, that mouth enveloping hers with strength and tenderness, shutting the whole world out for one heart-stopping moment.

Slowly, she swung her feet up onto the couch and lay back, her eyes misting with tears as she looked into the fire.

CHAPTER SIX

AFTER CHRIS had gone off in Ben's pickup the next morning, Jenny straightened the house and washed the breakfast dishes. Then she walked along the dirt road to the county highway where the mailboxes stood and opened the one marked Carmichael. A solitary letter was inside. She recognized her father's bold scrawl and tore it open:

> Jenny: Trust you didn't find things in too much disarray at the lake house. I was unable to reach Jack Preston. Grace and I have not been there since last summer, of course. We will be arriving Aug. 1 for a month.
>
> Father.

It was written on his office stationery. Carmichael, Sanders, Hoffmann and Braun. Despite the fact that it did indicate a microscopic amount of concern for her welfare, the note was more snub than comfort. Also, the not-so-subtle mention that they would be arriving on the first of August seemed a needless reminder that she and Chris were to be out before then. Jenny sighed and stuck it into the pocket of her jeans before walking slowly back toward the house.

Perhaps she should have made more of an effort to mend things with her father. But the first move, the

first step, had always seemed impossible. After Chris's
birth, she'd feared being rebuffed. Later, staying out of
his way had become so much a habit that she hardly
knew how to alter it. When she did think of it, her
fierce pride always sprang up with an argument. She
wasn't the only one, was she? *He* was capable of picking up the telephone, too. She followed his cases,
studying his arguments with great interest, but when,
occasionally, she glimpsed him outside a courtroom,
hurrying along with others around him, she turned
away quickly.

Jenny spent the rest of the day reading, catching up
on long overdue correspondence, even taking a chilly
swim in the lake. Then she straightened the guest house
and changed the sheets on the spare bed. While there
she again picked up the album she'd found in the storage room, feeling the same curiosity about who had
assembled it and why. This time she was more in control of her emotional reactions and lingered lovingly
over the pictures.

By the time the familiar pickup pulled up to the
kitchen door and Chris jumped out, she was beginning to feel anxious, wondering what the day had been
like for him. She held her breath, hoping that Ben
would get out, too, but he merely turned the truck
around and went back the way he had come. Jenny
swallowed her disappointment.

She'd roasted a chicken the way Chris liked, but he
seemed hardly aware of what he was eating when he sat
down at the table moments later. She could see that he
was sunburned, and something in the way he moved his
hands hinted at blisters.

"Well, how'd it go?" she asked, trying not to sound
too cheery.

"Okay."

"Same time tomorrow?"

"Uh-huh."

"Maybe we should put some bandages on your hands if they're blistered."

"They're okay," he said curtly, and Jenny fell silent.

The next day was a repetition of the first. Again, there was only a glimpse of Ben at the end of the day, and no wave or greeting. Chris, however, was slightly more talkative, less gloomy.

"We put in footings today. That's concrete you stick in a hole to hold up whatever it is you're building. Yesterday we mostly lugged the busted-up lumber to the dump."

"Have you met Mr. Hopworth?"

"Yeah. He's this old guy who raises a lot of vegetables out back of his house." Chris hesitated. "He got my letter. He came out and shook hands. He's not too bad."

"Well, it was a very good letter. I'm glad you're getting along."

"Ben said the footings weren't too great on the old shed. But he said maybe that was a good thing because if they had been, it wouldn't have cracked up so easy and might've wrecked the car more."

"Yes, I suppose that could be."

There was a pause and then he blurted, "I'm sorry I took the car the other night!"

Startled, Jenny said only, "Yes, I know you are."

On the third day it was Jenny who had a mishap. Straightening the kitchen shelves with their neat array of canned goods—all facing forward with labels showing, all arranged by categories—she heard an ominous groan, and suddenly the whole shelf collapsed on one side, sending cans crashing to the floor and rolling in every direction. A large can of corned-beef hash struck Jenny's toe and made her yelp with pain. She scurried to pick up the cans, muttering angrily to herself and thinking nervously of what her incredibly neat stepmother would say. She would have to get the thing fixed somehow.

Chris opened the screen door in the middle of it all, took a moment to register the chaos, and then asked, "What happened?"

Jenny explained, almost tearfully, hopping on one foot and massaging her injured toe, while Chris inspected the broken shelf.

"Well, no wonder. There's not enough support underneath to hold all that heavy stuff. Ben says that's one of the first rules in carpentry. I'll get a piece of wood from the shed. I can fix it."

"You can?" Jenny asked, staring at her son and forgetting about her toe.

"Sure." He said it casually.

He was back moments later. "I don't know if these nails are right, but they're all I could find." He was holding a length of two-by-four. "This ought to hold it up."

Jenny watched as he measured the rough brace and began pounding it in place.

"Where'd that hammer come from?" she asked.

"Ben gave it to me. He said a carpenter should have his own tools so he gets to know how they feel."

The reconstructed shelf held sturdily, and Jenny was able to rearrange its contents before they sat down to eat. She praised it, meaning every word, and regarded her son with new respect. Most of what she said seemed to pass over his head, however. He was at first preoccupied, then obviously exhausted, and before Jenny could set out the chocolate pudding she'd made for dessert, his eyelids were starting to droop.

They both overslept the next morning and were wakened by a horn blowing insistently outside. Chris, yanking on his jeans and T-shirt, went dashing out with his shoes in one hand, his hammer in the other.

"Chris! You haven't had breakfast! I haven't packed your lunch!" Jenny called after him.

"It's okay, Mom. Gotta go," he yelled back.

"I'll bring you something!" she shouted as the truck wheeled around. She had only a glimpse of Ben at the wheel, one tanned arm resting on the windowsill.

Why hadn't he stopped at all during the past three days? As she turned back into the house and went about dressing, her mind kept returning to him. He was certainly determined to engage Chris's interest and keep him working at the building. But of course he was doing that for Chris, not for her. Suddenly he seemed to have no interest in her whatsoever. Well, how could she blame him, after the way she'd spoken to him, accusing him of all sorts of... Jenny blushed, just thinking about it. But he'd kissed her. The blush deepened as she remembered that kiss and admitted to herself that this wasn't the first time she'd thought of it. Countless times during the day and just before sleep claimed her it came back to her, as well as her own response to it. Over and over she'd felt the warm insistent pressure of his lips and let her mind drift to an enchantment of speculation about deeper involvement. Had it been only a casual thing to him? Something with no significance at all?

I'm going to marry Philip. She heard the words in her head, and then she spoke them aloud, repeating them clearly for her own benefit. Thinking about anything else was ridiculous. She marched into the kitchen and made coffee, feeling a moment's worry about a lanky twelve-year-old starting off to do a day's hard work without any breakfast. And in the next moment the worry was gone. Ben would look after him.

Despite all the internal arguments she used to bolster her own courage, it began to fail her as she packed a lunch for Chris late in the morning. She found herself opening the refrigerator and staring blankly at its interior, tearing waxed paper crookedly off the roll, looking nervously at the kitchen clock.

What would she say to Ben when she saw him again? Would he be cold and distant? More than likely. And if he was, how should she react? Her hands were chilly with apprehension as she got in the car.

She needn't have worried, Jenny realized the moment she pulled up in front of Mr. Hopworth's property. Both Ben and Chris waved to her from the floor of the small skeletal structure where framing studs were just being raised. When Ben approached her as she got out of the car, his smile was wide and welcoming. Jenny felt an enormous wash of relief, but at the same time a more distant, prickling stab of disappointment. It was so casual and offhand, the greeting the sort he'd have given anyone.

"So you've come to inspect the project," he said. He was shirtless, his faded jeans riding low on his lean hips. The dark hair on his chest tapered to a V at the waist of his jeans. Close to him, she could see the faintest trace of sweat on his skin, like the bloom on a grape. It would taste salty, she thought, and then clamped down hard on the image and said brightly, "I've heard lots of good things about it. Actually, I brought lunch. I can't imagine what made us both oversleep this morning. I should have set my alarm, but I didn't realize I'd need it...."

Stop chattering, she ordered herself.

He turned and called, "Chris, how about giving your mother the grand tour? Show her what we're doing."

"Sure." He jumped down and came over to them. Both dogs were at his heels. He had taken his shirt off, too.

"Did you starve this morning?" she asked as he joined them.

"Nope, we went to McDonald's. Ben said you can't work on an empty stomach."

"Oh, I am sorry," she said.

"It's okay." Ben smiled, dismissing it. "Now, come take a look at this creation of ours."

Chris was explaining it all with enthusiasm. "Once we get the studs up, we can do the roof. See, we've got three sides done, but in the front it's got to be different, because that's got to be open and have a counter. We're going to build a door over the counter that comes down at night to close it all up. Daytimes it'll be open and fastened to the ceiling with a hook."

"It looks like a very professional job," she said admiringly.

"Ben built a room on his house," Chris explained. "He knows about all that stuff."

"Well, not all," Ben objected mildly. "But trial and error can teach you a lot."

"When it's done, maybe by the end of the week, we're going to paint it," Chris explained.

"Mr. Hopworth's gone to buy that now, in fact," Ben said. "He told us he'd been planning to paint the old stand, anyway, so it was only fair that he buy the paint for the new one, which was pretty generous of him, I thought."

"Hey, here he comes now," Chris said.

A pickup truck slightly shabbier than Ben's turned into the unpaved driveway that sloped upward toward a modest white frame house. At the crest it stopped and an elderly man got out and walked down to greet them.

"How do," he said, lifting a hand in greeting. He was thin and wiry, his trousers riding high, his white shirt tieless but buttoned all the way up. "You must be Chris's mother. Real glad to meet you."

"This is Mr. Hopworth," Ben said.

Jenny shook hands with him and asked if he was pleased with the new stand.

"Pleased! Best thing that's happened this year, getting rid of that old one." His laughter wheezed jovially. "These two fellers are doing a bang-up job, too."

"It looks fine to me," Jenny agreed.

"How about the paint?" Ben asked. "What did you pick?"

"It's called Desert Sand," the old man said seriously. "Gotta little pink to it, but not too much, mind. I just liked the looks of it. Chris, boy, why don't you run up and fetch it outta the truck?"

Chris went up the slope and lowered the tailgate on the old truck, took out two buckets and slammed the tailgate shut. Then he headed back toward them.

Watching him, Jenny wondered whether it was her imagination or whether he really did look stronger and more confident than he had three days ago. Suddenly she heard a wobbly, grating sound, and behind Chris the old truck began to move backward. In the same instant there was a burst of noise and energy as Blaze snarled and rushed at the boy. The dog lunged at him and knocked him out of the way. Jenny screamed as Chris sprawled on the grass with the dog standing over him. Ben made a dash for the truck, which was slowly rolling down the slope. In one smooth motion, he opened the door, leapt into the cab and slammed on the brake. When it was secured he jumped down and came back to where Jenny was on her knees beside Chris.

"Everybody okay?" he asked.

Chris was already sitting up, looking slightly bewildered. Mr. Hopworth rushed to join them.

"Golly damn, what'd I do, Ben? Didn't put her in gear, I'll bet."

"Afraid that's it, Mr. Hopworth."

"You all right, boy?" the old man asked with concern.

"I'm fine," Chris said, and looked around for Blaze, who was sitting calmly a few feet away. The dog edged over to him, and Chris threw an arm around his neck. Jenny stood up, trembling from head to foot, and managed a smile. A thought popped crazily into her head. *I've been scared of that dog from the first moment I saw him. So much for my good judgment.*

Mr. Hopworth still looked worried as Chris scrambled to his feet. "I oughtta be stood up and shot, I reckon."

"Nah," Chris said, brushing himself off. "Just an accident." He grinned at Mr. Hopworth. "Now we're even."

Ben put an arm lightly around Jenny's shoulders. "How about unpacking that lunch now? Chris is probably ready for a break.'' They walked together to her car, Jenny's legs still wobbly.

"I'm sorry I screamed," she murmured. She could feel through her cotton shirt the warmth of his hand on her shoulder. "I just didn't know what was going on. The dog scared me."

"Those two have really hit it off," Ben said. "Blaze hasn't ever taken to anybody before—not like that."

Jenny nodded and reached inside the car for the lunch she'd packed. He was being thoughtful and concerned, she thought, but that's all it was. Polite, the way he'd be with anybody. At once she scolded herself. What was she expecting, anyway—sighs and deep meaningful looks? Whispers and words of love meant just for her? What world was she living in, anyway?

"I packed plenty of sandwiches," she said. "Maybe you'll help Chris finish them."

Late in the day when he brought Chris home in the pickup, he went home as usual without glancing toward the house.

It was almost nine when she heard the knock at the back door. The last of the sunlight had dropped away, and she could see only a tall shadowy form there.

"Hi," a familiar voice said. "Am I calling too late? I brought something for Chris."

Jenny's heart slammed against her ribs and her pulse raced. She did her best to keep her voice even as she walked to the door.

"Not too late at all, except that Chris has been in bed for thirty minutes, and I'm sure he's been asleep for twenty-nine of them." She pushed open the door. "Come on in. Is it something I can pass along to him?"

"Sure. It's a book." He came in, ducking slightly as if not sure his height would clear the doorway. "I spoke to him about it, and I thought he might like to read it."

"I was just sitting on the porch," she said. "It's the first night it's been warm enough."

"Enjoy it then," he said. "It won't last."

The kitchen was dark, but light streamed in from the living room. It picked out the planes of his face, but threw his eyes into shadow so that she was unable to read their expression. She felt a curious unsteadiness in her body, as if nerves and muscles were operating outside her control.

"Won't you come and sit, too?" she asked, and he followed her through the living room and onto the porch. Here, too, there was faint light from the room behind them, and the night itself held a luminous quality so that the lake looked silvered.

"The moon's going to be full tonight," he said, and then added with a grin, "That's what brought me out."

Fireflies were darting through the darkness, and from the water came the loon's cry. Jenny sat on the porch step, and he dropped down beside her. In front of them the land fell away steeply toward the lake.

"What book is it?" she asked, hoping he couldn't hear the way her heart was thumping.

"My grandfather wrote it," he said, and handed it to her. "He was something of an authority on this part of the country. It's about fly-fishing, of course, but also wilderness survival and basic carpentry."

"Is he the one who taught you?" Jenny held the book, still warm from his hands.

"He and my dad both. But having to do it is when you really learn."

"Well, Chris certainly seems to be learning." She told him about the broken shelf. "The repair may be a little primitive, but I bet that shelf will outlast the house." She saw his smile and went on hesitantly, "You were right about Chris and what he needed, you know. I've never seen him so happy. I've always worried about him because I felt he missed a lot."

He turned to her. "Doesn't he ever see his father?"

"No, never. I don't even know where he is now." She turned the book in her hands. "And of course he's never known his grandfather."

"Why 'of course'?"

"Well ... I don't know. Families seem to splinter nowadays."

"Only if you let them," he suggested gently.

"It isn't as easy as just saying it. And it isn't all our fault, either. My father isn't... It's hard to talk to him. About anything important."

Ben nodded slowly, but offered no comment, and for several minutes there was silence between them. A soft wind made the pines around the porch rustle. Suddenly, surprising herself, Jenny broke the quiet by saying, "Philip slept in the guest house when he was here, you know." The moment the words were out she bit her lip.

If she'd taken him unawares he didn't show it. He waited a moment to answer and then said, "I guess I knew that. Not at first, maybe, but when I'd taken the time to think about it."

Jenny took a breath, felt it catch in her throat. "Why?"

"Oh, because I think that's the kind of woman you are."

"You don't know what kind of woman I am," she whispered.

He gave a low laugh. "Sure I do. I know you're sensitive and caring. I know you worry too much. I know what your son means to you, and I know you'd never do anything that you thought might hurt him. Also—" a faint note of amusement crept into his voice "—you're Buzz Carmichael's daughter, whether you like the idea or not."

"What on earth does that mean?"

"Oh, that you're a little straitlaced, perhaps. You were taught good manners, and you used to wear white gloves when you went to Miss McAllister's dancing school in Boston. You did go there, didn't you?" She could hear the teasing note again.

"Yes, but how did...?"

"I've lived in Boston. I know how these things work."

Feeling slightly indignant, she said, "I really don't see what possible connection..." She paused and started over, a bit more diffidently, "I'm not always straitlaced."

He looked at her in the dim light for several seconds. Then he kissed her softly, their lips clinging for a moment. "I know you're not," he said. "But you have an agenda. A life plan."

She tried to keep her voice level, to keep the unsteadiness out of it. "You say that as if there's something wrong with it. I mean, what's so bad about trying to keep some order in your life? And having a long-range plan does give you something to work toward. Certainly Chris needs that."

"And what do you need?" he asked softly.

"I don't know what you mean." She could hear her own voice, slightly indignant and schoolgirlish.

"Well, Chris isn't the only one to be considered here."

"But he's my responsibility."

"Is that why you're marrying Philip? Because it'll be good for Chris?"

"I don't—I didn't mean—That's not the only consideration, of course."

"Oh, no. I forgot. There are those two parallel careers. Two briefcases on the hall table, two answering machines, those lively discussions about torts and contracts over the breakfast table."

She gave a little gasp of anger, but before she could answer him he stood up and said, "Come on. Let's go out."

Still fuming, she let him pull her to her feet. "Go out? Where?"

"Out on the lake. In the canoe."

"Now?"

"There's a sensational moon—it'd be a crime to waste it."

"But Chris will be here alone. I don't know if I should..."

He led the way through the house to the back door, where two dark figures waited on the doorstep.

"Rocket might not rise to an emergency, but I think we can count on Blaze, don't you?"

"I'm sure we can," she admitted.

The night was full of a pale brightness from the moon, which was now visible over the tops of the tall pines. Once, as they made their way down the path toward the water, she stepped uncertainly. Ben's hand steadied her and stayed on her arm the rest of the way.

Jenny felt as if she had entered into a world different
from the daytime world where everything was known
and recognizable. Here objects were black and silver,
an arrangement of shapes and outlines totally new to
her. The lake, spread in a metallic sheet before them,
was streaked by a long silver path where the moon's
reflection lay.

The amiable Rocket tagged along after them, but
Blaze had not stirred from the doorstep. Now Ben sent
the other dog back and held the canoe steady so Jenny
could get in. Then he untied the line and stepped into
the stern.

"Will you be a passenger or do you want to paddle,
too?" he asked.

"I'll paddle, of course," she said, a hint of indignation in her tone.

"Oh, I forgot." He sighed. "You always pull your
own weight."

"Is there something wrong with—" He quickly
broke in. "No no. Don't be so quick to look for hid-
den meanings."

I'm being ridiculous, Jenny thought. *Why can't I
just relax and be myself?* Was it because she seemed to
become another self when she was with him? A Jenny
she almost failed to recognize sometimes?

Still, some of the things he had said on the porch
were swimming around in her head.

"It's all very well for you to look down your nose at
making plans and choices," she said over her shoulder
as he pushed away from the dock with his paddle and
then started stroking smoothly through the water.
"You've always belonged here in this place and you
knew what you wanted. It was easy for you to choose.
I mean, it couldn't have been any choice at all."

With her back to him, she had no idea what his expression was, but his voice was half-amused as he said, "Well, now, that's where you're wrong, Madam Prosecutor. I've made plans that went wrong and I've also made some fairly important decisions. Important to me, that is."

"What kind of decisions?" she asked suspiciously. She had picked up her paddle and was stroking earnestly.

"Someday I'll tell you."

"Not tonight?"

"No, not tonight. We're not supposed to talk about such things out here on the lake."

"Oh? Who says?"

"Me. Sullivan's Law. We're supposed to be quiet and look around and let the night talk to us. We do the listening."

Feeling properly chastised, Jenny settled back to her paddling. In the silence she began to hear sounds and notice details she'd been unaware of. There was the steady thrust and whisper of Ben's paddle behind her, and the flash of silver of her own paddle when the moon caught its dripping blade just before she plunged it into the water again. There was the familiar call of a loon somewhere nearby, and the thousand small sounds along the shoreline of creatures scurrying on their night missions. High up on the right, silhouetted against the moonlight, she could see the ragged outline of the osprey's nest. Somewhere out in the middle of the lake there was another flash of silver and then a plop as a fish jumped.

Quietly they paddled to the beach where they'd picnicked. How long ago? Only a little more than a week. Yet it seemed to Jenny longer than that. It didn't seem possible that she'd known Ben Sullivan such a short time. Not that she knew him well. She hardly knew him at all. And his cryptic remarks indicated there was much more to him. Yet she already felt as if he had slid into a place in her life that would seem empty once she returned to Boston.

With an effort she brought herself back to concentrating on the lake and the night and the steady rhythm of the two paddles dipping and rising together. She felt as if every stroke took her farther and farther from Philip and the life she had left behind in Boston. The moon-drenched night was a fantasy world, but it was also a place that would be gone tomorrow. You couldn't count on fantasies or dreams or make-believe. All you could do was enjoy them while they lasted.

She became aware that Ben was turning the canoe back toward the dock, which was now far behind them. Jenny wanted to tell him not to. She could hardly bear to have this interlude of beauty and peace end. But she was too shy to say the words to him, so she stayed silent as the canoe swung around. Then he stopped paddling, letting them drift silently only a short distance out from land.

Suddenly he whispered, "Shh. Be very still. Look over there on the shore. Where that rock juts out. There's a big pine to the right. Do you see him?"

Him? Jenny looked hard and then saw movement as a moose lowered his great antlered head to drink from the lake. She nodded without saying a word and felt her breath catch in her throat at the sight. They sat in silence and watched as the head came up again, the antlers etched darkly against the pale moonlight. He stood for a long time, dipping his head to drink, then raising it and finally lumbering off with a kind of clumsy majesty.

Jenny let her breath out. "Is he the one you told me about?"

"Yes. Sometimes you don't see him all summer."

"How can you tell he's the one?"

"I can't." There was a smile in his voice. "I just like to think so." He began paddling again, heading toward the dock. "That makes tonight special."

"I thought it was special even before that," Jenny said. "Now it's something else—magical."

"I'm glad you saw him."

They said no more, and soon they were at the dock. He helped her out, then made the canoe fast before turning to where she waited. His arms came around her without a moment's hesitation, pressing her close to him, and neither of them seemed to need words. It was a continuation of the dream, Jenny thought as she lifted up her face and felt his mouth on hers once more. She clung to him, answering his kiss with her own, feeling her body mold itself to his. In the symphony of a thousand small night noises, she could hear the steady beating of his heart and her own answering it.

It wouldn't last, she reminded herself. It would evaporate like this night of dreams and magic. She was going to marry Philip. She was going back to Boston at the end of the month. Her father's terse note had reminded her of that. And once she was back there she would never see Ben Sullivan again.

CHAPTER SEVEN

JENNY STAYED AWAY from the construction site for the next few days. The less she saw of Ben, she reasoned, the safer she would be. She suspected his thoughts were traveling along the same path, for he steered clear of the house except for picking up Chris and bringing him home. Half wishing he would stop each time the truck rolled into the driveway, Jenny felt herself pulled in two anguished directions. She tried to overcome this by keeping busy. She took long walks, swam, wrote letters, started reading her way through the pile of books she'd brought and tried new recipes, which Chris pronounced highly successful.

"I really can't take that as a compliment," she told him. "These days you're hungry enough to eat wallpaper spread with library paste."

"Yuck," Chris said.

She counted off the days on the calendar, realizing suddenly that their vacation was sliding away fast. She noted the date coming up Saturday and decided to keep quiet about it. Her birthday was the last thing she felt like celebrating this year.

But on Saturday morning Chris tiptoed into her bedroom.

"Hey, Mom, are you awake?" he whispered.

Jenny, who was, but only barely, opened one eye and peered at her son. "I am now. What's up? I didn't know you were working today."

"We're not. The stand's done. Remember, I told you last night we'd finished painting it?" He was already dressed, she noted.

"Oh. Right. Well, you're up pretty early then."

"Yeah, I know. But as long as you're awake, why don't you come out to the kitchen?"

She had both eyes open now, and suppressed excitement was clearly visible on his face.

"Okay. Let me put some clothes on and splash a little water on my face."

"Hurry up."

He disappeared, and Jenny threw back the covers.

When she'd pulled on her jeans and sweatshirt and swiped at her hair with a brush, she padded out to the kitchen in her bare feet. Chris was standing beside the table, moving from one foot to the other. On the table was a square slatted box, neatly beveled at the corners, open at the top and varnished to a warm shine.

"Happy birthday!" Chris exploded. "I made it."

Jenny circled the table, still not sure what the box was, but sensing its importance to Chris.

"It's beautiful!" she exclaimed.

"Bet you don't know what it is."

Recognition dawned suddenly. "Of course I do," Jenny said. "It's a planter."

"Right! You put a plant in there, pot and all."

She gave him a hug. "Best-looking one I ever saw," she said. "And imagine you remembering my birthday."

"That's not all," he said, disentangling himself. "We're going to have a party. Well, sort of a party. Just as soon as Ben gets here."

"Ben..." Jenny's face bloomed with heat, and the old uncontrollable racing of her heart started up.

"Sure. He helped me make the planter. I mean, not helped me really, but he showed me how to make it. So we planned this thing to do today, and that's why I woke you, because we have to start out early."

As if on cue, the familiar sound of the pickup came from outside. Jenny, unable to move, stood by the table while Chris flung open the door. Ben entered, invisible at first behind a large green fern.

"Happy birthday," he said, depositing the fern in the new planter. He smiled at her and kissed her lightly on the cheek.

Jenny struggled to stay cool and casual. "Goodness, if I'd known all this was going to happen I'd have set my alarm and tried to look halfway presentable for the occasion."

"You look absolutely perfect," Ben assured her softly. "And I assume you're ready for the next event?"

"I might be if I knew what it was," she said. The soft touch of his lips on her cheek was still with her.

"Oh, no. This is a surprise all the way." He and Chris exchanged looks, and Jenny put both hands on her hips and regarded them severely.

"Fine, but how do I dress for it?"

"Just like that," Chris put in eagerly.

"Except with shoes," Ben added, glancing down at her bare feet.

"Give me five minutes," she begged.

Chris frowned impatiently, but Ben said, "Take ten if you need them. I'll make some coffee."

Jenny hurried back to her bedroom, feeling just the way she had on Christmas mornings years ago when her mother was alive. She hurried to put on socks and Reeboks, gave her hair a better brushing and added a light touch of lipstick. She smoothed her bed hastily, looked around the room and hurried back to the kitchen. Color had come into her cheeks and her eyes were bright with anticipation. It was her birthday, after all, she reminded her more sensible, cautious self. It was only one day out of the year. It was all right, wasn't it, to enjoy your birthday?

"Ready," she said breathlessly.

Across the room, Ben poured her a mug of coffee. His eyes swept over her. She could see how they crinkled at the corners.

"Sure you're ready for anything?" he asked.

Jenny didn't speak, but nodded slowly. The silence was thick with unspoken words between them. Then Chris, fidgeting and impatient, said, "Well, okay. Let's get started, for Pete's sake."

They struck off on foot through the woods, following a path that led away from the lake for a distance, then circled back toward it so that now and then they could glimpse the water. Ben led the way, with Jenny following and Chris bringing up the rear with the two dogs. The path was not well-worn, and in spots it was overgrown. Ben walked with easy assurance, and Jenny kept her eyes on his broad back, watching the play of muscles under his denim shirt.

"No one's been this way lately, have they?" she asked.

"Not much, certainly, and some of the storms last winter really messed it up." He paused where a pine had fallen across the path. "I'll have to come back with a chain saw, but for now we can just climb over." He turned to her and before she could protest, seized her by the waist and lifted her lightly over the log. Jenny gave a surprised gasp, and he grinned as he put her down and started walking again.

"But where are we?" she asked. "Whose property are we on?"

"Mine, actually," he said over his shoulder. "Farther along we'll get closer to the lake."

"It's all in the book," Chris said behind her.

"The book?" Jenny glanced back at him, and for the space of a second had the odd impression that it was a stranger walking behind her, not thin, nervous Chris who bit his nails and sat mesmerized by television hour after hour. This was a tanned, strong boy who seemed to have acquired muscle and poise he'd never possessed before.

"You know, the book Ben brought me. The one his grandfather wrote."

"Oh. What's this thing he wrote about?"

"You'll see."

"This is turning out to be a very mysterious birthday," she complained, but it wasn't a real complaint, and everyone knew it. She was freer and happier than she'd been in years, and the crisp morning air of the pine-scented woods woke an unexpected joy in her. Their destination mattered not at all, as long as she could keep walking along in Ben's footsteps, watching his smooth stride, holding out her hand and feeling the sudden warm contact as he reached back to help her over a rough spot in the path.

After a half hour or so they came to a clearing in the woods. Sunlight was streaming through the opening in the trees, and Jenny saw that they had indeed swung back in the direction of the lake so that the water lay before them only a stone's throw away, sparkling and alive in the bright morning air. In the center of the clearing stood a small log house.

"Is that it?" Chris called out excitedly, running ahead for a better look.

"That's it." Ben stood with his hands on his hips, smiling at Jenny.

Her glance swung around the clearing, and she took in the snug little house that seemed to nestle close to the ground.

"Whose house is it?" she asked softly.

"My grandfather's," he said. "Well, I suppose it's mine now, but I always think of it as his. He built it, with my dad and me helping out."

"It's all in that book Ben loaned me," Chris said breathlessly, coming back to them. "His name was Ben, too. Well, Bennett, actually. He called it his fishing cabin. And that's where he wrote the book. He wrote about how you build one, too."

So his name is Bennett, Jenny was thinking. And once he was a boy like Chris, helping his grandfather right here in this clearing. She tried to imagine that youthful Ben, following orders, concentrating hard, his sharp young mind storing away everything he learned.

"It's beautiful," she breathed, walking to the front door. Instead of a handle, there was a twisted knob of wood that had been a branch or perhaps part of a tree root. Worn smooth from handling, it felt warm to the touch.

"Lift," Ben said, and Jenny lifted. A latch moved and the door swung open. She stood on the doorstep looking inside, aware that he was standing just behind her. His hands came up to rest lightly on her shoulders and Jenny shuddered in delight. Then the moment was broken by Chris's enthusiastic cry. "Hey, that's neat! Look at that, Mom!"

"Come on, let's go in," Ben said lightly.

It was one room, about sixteen feet square, with a stone fireplace, two small windows facing the water, a cot for sleeping and a plain plank table. Against the wall were shelves to hold supplies. Hooks for clothing were fashioned out of sturdy sections of tree branches.

Jenny turned slowly, taking it all in. Chris darted from one spot to another, touching and exclaiming, "Hey, look at this, Mom! I read about this in the book! You know something? They cut the logs for it right here."

Jenny looked at Ben for confirmation. He nodded.

"That's how we made the clearing."

"Beautiful," Jenny repeated, her eyes going over the rough walls, the simple furnishings.

After a moment Ben said, "Look, we've got all day to explore the place. Chris, you'd better get busy. Who knows what kind of luck you're going to have, and we're going to be mighty hungry before long. Rod's over there in the corner. Flies on the shelf above."

When he had gone out carrying the fishing gear, the dogs at his heels, Jenny asked, "You're counting on Chris to catch our meal?"

"Why not? If his luck runs bad we'll try another spot and I'll join in. But my guess is he'll do all right. The worst that can happen is we'll go hungry. Besides, I cheated just a little." The dark eyes sparkled as he drew a package out from under his shirt. "Bacon," he said in a conspiratorial whisper, tossing it on the table.

Jenny shook her head in disbelief, and both of them laughed. He took a step toward her and she moved toward him, and suddenly his arms were around her, warm and strong, his lips seeking hers. Arguments, self-doubt, questioning, uncertainty, all melted away as she felt herself drawn into the circle of his desire, her own matching and answering it. Once again, as on the night they'd gone out on the lake, she felt as if they were moving in a world apart from the world she'd always known. His mouth caressed hers, his kisses probed deeper. Her arms, circling his neck, pulled him closer.

When they parted, both of them breathless, she still clung to him, her face pressed against his shoulder. "I've never felt—I mean, I can't believe— None of this seems real."

"It doesn't get any more real than this," he said close to her ear. His breath was warm and stirred her hair. "But right now—" reluctantly he pulled away from her "—we have to build a fire." He hesitated and smiled down at her. "Another fire, perhaps I should say." They kissed again, softly.

They built it outside in the clearing. "We could use the fireplace in the cabin," he said. "But a day like this we can do our cooking outdoors."

"Have you always lived here at Tucker's Pond?" she asked. She was sitting cross-legged on the ground watching him. Down at the water's edge, they could see Chris casting his line with the two dogs observing critically.

"No, I lived in Augusta. But we were here a good part of every year. Grandfather owned property here, and so did my parents."

"Where are they now?"

"Grandfather's gone, and my parents are retired but active. Still in Augusta, but inching a bit farther south every winter."

"Any of them lawyers?"

"All of them." He smiled. "Including my mother."

"Really?" Jenny was astounded, seeing him in a different light. She'd pictured him as a self-sufficient loner, but now suddenly she could see him as part of a lively, challenging clan. "Any brothers or sisters?"

"One brother. A renegade. He's in the foreign service. In the Middle East right now."

Jenny frowned slightly, thinking back. "That night you came to the house—the night we went out in the canoe—you mentioned that you'd lived in Boston. And later you said you'd had some difficult decisions to make. Did you practice law in Boston, by any chance?"

Ben carefully added a log to the fire.

"I did. For a while. I was with Gunderson and Lathrop."

Jenny noted the name of the prestigious firm with surprise, but said nothing.

"Everything was going along fine and I was on the fast track to becoming a partner, when one day it occurred to me I wasn't having much fun. I missed Maine, the people I knew here, the way life was lived. What I was doing was lucrative and all that, but it wasn't making me happy. So I quit."

Philip would never have left. The thought sprang into Jenny's mind unexpectedly.

"But do you find—I mean, is there enough to challenge you here? How do you keep busy?"

He shot her a grin. "You mean you figure it must get dull sentencing the occasional Saturday-night drunk or settling disputes about whose apple tree is on the property line?"

"Well, yes, something like that."

"The judge business—that's temporary. Old Judge Hurley died in January and I was appointed to finish out his term. And actually, I don't find it dull. The law is the law, on whatever level, and it's all fascinating to me. But I have a practice, as well, and I'd rather concentrate on that, so when this term's over later in the year I'll be going back to it."

"But even that. Tucker's Pond can't have very many legal tangles."

"My practice is a little larger than just Tucker's Pond," he said quietly. "I get clients from quite a big area. And I lecture at the university law school from time to time. Also, since I parted amicably from my old firm in Boston, they give me a call when they think I might be helpful." He paused. "I'm not completely out of touch."

Jenny stared at him, trying to reconcile the picture of the man working on old Mr. Hopworth's vegetable stand, shirtless and sweating in the summer sun, with the attorney whose reputation was obviously noteworthy enough that he was invited to lecture and was consulted when difficult cases came up.

"It's a whole different you," she said softly. "I can't quite take it in."

He walked around the fire, which was now blazing briskly, and reached down to pull her to her feet.

"Does it make a difference?" he asked, searching her face.

"No, of course not. I have to get used to it, that's all."

"Perhaps we could speed that along."

He bent to kiss her again, both his hands cradling her head, his strong fingers tangling in her hair.

"Hey! I got one!"

The jubilant cry parted them, but their eyes stayed on each other for a moment before they looked down toward the water where Chris was reeling in a respectable-sized fish.

"Perhaps we'd better join him and offer congratulations," Ben suggested. They strolled down to the lake and admired the bass he'd caught.

"How many more do you think we need?" the boy asked.

"Maybe two," Ben said, and Chris gave a confident shrug.

"No problem," he said. He glanced curiously from Ben to his mother before turning back to fasten a fly on his line.

The fish were cleaned and filleted, rolled in cornmeal and fried in bacon fat over the open fire. Rocket and Blaze stayed close to the action, noses twitching in anticipation.

"Now where did that cornmeal come from?" Jenny demanded, licking her fingers and tackling another piece of fish.

"I was here a couple of weeks ago," Ben said. "Straightening the place up a little and laying in a few supplies. I try to keep staples here during the summer."

"This is the most delicious fish I've ever eaten," she said. "Positively."

"There's the man to thank," Ben said, nodding toward Chris. "He could've cooked it, too, except that I took pity on him."

"That's right, Mom, I could've," Chris said. "It's all in the book that the other Ben wrote. And how to build a fire when it's wet out. You can find dry grass and stuff underneath where a log's fallen. And if you peel wet sticks they'll be dry underneath. Only you should always carry matches with you in a tin box or something like that." He gave scraps to the two dogs, who were seated at his elbows, as he spoke. "There's even things you can eat if you don't have food. Dandelions and a lot of other stuff. He drew pictures of them. Birch bark's good to eat, too."

"I believe you, but I'm glad I didn't have to eat dandelions and birch bark on my birthday," Jenny said with a laugh. "Is there any more of that fish?"

They brought water from the lake to wash the dishes when they were done, let the fire die down and for a long time simply sat basking in the sun. They took an exploratory walk through the surrounding woods, with Chris plunging ahead, shouting over each discovery.

Close to each other, Jenny and Ben walked in silence for the most part, hands touching occasionally. Birds were noisy in the trees above them, and sun filtered through the branches.

"You never said anything about love when you told me about your life," Jenny said at last. "Wasn't there somebody, sometime?"

He gave her a quick glance and then looked away. "There was somebody once."

Even though she had asked the question, Jenny felt her heart sink.

"Someone you knew in Boston?" It was like probing a sensitive tooth, but she couldn't help it.

"Yes. She was a medical student then. Now she's a doctor. She had a very good offer from a hospital in New Mexico, which she wanted to take. And I wanted her to take it, of course. It was a great opportunity for her. But my roots were here and I couldn't see myself leaving, so we parted."

"That's all there was to it?"

He gave a low laugh. "Well, no, I suppose there was more, but that's the essence. Anyway, I have enormous respect for her. She's a good person."

Jenny nodded, thinking that it was like Ben to say that, to be fair, no matter what. She sensed that he was never less than fair.

They reentered the clearing, checked the fire's ashes and threw water on them, took a last look at the cabin and then, with the sun sinking lower, began the walk back.

"This is the best birthday I've ever had," Jenny said, taking the hand that Ben held out to help her over a log.

"Oh, but it's not over yet," he said.

"What do you mean? How could we possibly top this?" Jenny trudged along in his wake with Chris bringing up the rear. The two dogs ranged beside them, rooting through fallen leaves and poking their noses into clumps of ferns.

"We're going out to dinner tonight. All of us."

"Dinner! I'm still full from lunch."

"You won't be after the hike back. I'll give you a chance to catch your breath first. I have to take the dogs home, anyway."

"But where are we going?"

"A place the locals know but the tourists don't," he said. "Mrs. McCracken's place in town. She cooks on order only, so I have my order in."

"Hey, you guys..." Chris, who had been listening, sounded hesitant. They stopped walking and turned to him.

"The thing is...uh, I guess I should've said something before, but Mrs. Hazelton invited me over there because her grandson's coming to spend the night and she's going to let us put up a tent and camp outside." He looked troubled. "So I won't be able to go with you to that place."

Ben looked at Jenny. "It's up to your mom," he said.

"Oh, Chris, you go ahead. You've given me a wonderful day already."

"Gee. Okay, that's great."

They continued walking, and Jenny's thoughts tumbled wildly over each other. A real date, she told herself, feeling like a teenager. Just the two of them.

"I have to dress up," she said.

He turned to glance at her with something like amusement in his eyes. "I assure you, it's not required at Mrs. McCracken's."

"But it's my birthday, and I intend to."

"Okay, fine. Say I pick you up around seven. That's fashionably late for Tucker's Pond."

"Seven will be fine."

The ancient Plymouth came clanking into the driveway shortly before six. A light-haired boy of about

Chris's age was with Adele, and he and Chris shook hands in a manly, if slightly self-conscious fashion. He was shorter than Chris, and stockier, but his smile was broad and good-natured, and Jenny guessed they'd hit it off. She thanked Adele and waved them out of sight before turning back and heading for the shower. Her insides were a jumble of excitement, anticipation and apprehension, but her eyes, when she glanced the mirror, were dancing with amber lights.

She drew a deep breath, trying to relax, but every muscle was tingling, every nerve fine-tuned to an exhilaration she hadn't felt in years. She stepped into the shower and let the hot water pound her into relaxation. She shampooed her hair and rinsed it luxuriously. She had a whole hour to collect herself, she reminded her impatient self. She wanted to appear calm and in control, not flighty and shallow the way she so often felt in the face of Ben's calm decisiveness. Stepping out of the shower and wrapping her head in a towel, she pulled on a terry-cloth robe and inspected the dress hanging on the back of the door.

It was the only dress she'd brought with her—a green cotton knit that went well with her coloring. Not elegant evening wear, but it was all she had, and in Tucker's Pond it might be perfect. For a moment Jenny stood absolutely still in the steamy little bathroom and crossed her arms, hugging herself in joyous anticipation. She'd been alone with Ben before, but never when the object was simply to have a good time together. She squeezed her eyes shut, letting her mind run ahead to the evening before them.

She heard a distant pounding at the kitchen door.

Jenny's eyes flew open. It couldn't possibly be seven yet! And here she was with her head in a towel, not nearly ready. She tightened the belt of her robe, hung on to the towel and went dashing out of the bathroom. Well, he'd seen her plenty of other times when she wasn't exactly at her best, she thought philosophically.

"I thought you said seven..." she was scolding good-naturedly as she hurried into the kitchen and stopped short in front of the screen door. Her eyes took in the three figures standing outside.

"Philip!"

"Surprise!" came the chorus from three voices. And then Philip begged, "Open this thing, for heaven's sake, Jenny. We're loaded down with goodies. You remember Craig and Tina, don't you?"

CHAPTER EIGHT

JENNY FELT HERSELF trembling as she hurried to open the door. She recognized the other man. Craig Downing, an attorney, a friend of Philip's. And the woman, Tina something... Jenny had a vague memory of meeting her at a party once.

"Hello, darling." Philip bent to kiss her cheek. "You didn't think I'd miss your birthday, did you? I talked these two into coming so it'd be more of a party." He was carrying two bottles of champagne in the crook of his arm. With his free hand he was holding one handle of a large hamper. Craig, shorter than Philip and with slightly thinning hair, was holding the other. Jennie managed a nod and a smile in his direction. As they made for the table with their burden, Jenny snatched up the planter with the fern and set it carefully on the counter. She felt close to tears.

"Philip, really, you should have let me know," she said.

"Absolutely not. This had to be a surprise," Philip said. With his arms free he seized her and spun her around in a tight hug. Tina, a small dark-haired woman in black tights and a voluminous flowered smock, gave her an impulsive embrace when he'd released her.

"Happy Birthday, Jeanie," she said gleefully, and Jenny didn't correct her. Tina was carrying an enor-

mous bag, as well as a wicker hamper. "Wait till you
see what we've brought. It's all from that new restaurant—what's the name of it, Craig? Bellisario's? Absolutely wonderful place—everybody's going there
now. We've brought ceviche made with shrimp and
scallops. And this marvelous veal thing—"

"*Veal involtini,*" Craig supplied. "You know, that
sounds vaguely illegal?" He laughed heartily and
Philip joined in.

"No, actually it's wonderful," Philip assured her.
"It's got prosciutto in it and provolone, and they do it
with this puff pastry—you'll love it. But first we'd
better put the champagne on ice. We'll want to start off
with that."

The kitchen was suddenly full of clutter, noise,
voices, movement. Jenny's heart had turned to a cold
block of ice.

"If I'd only known you were coming," she said
weakly, and Philip turned a radiant smile on her.
"Darling, stop fussing now. Of course if you'd known
we were coming you wouldn't have come rushing out
here like a wet puppy. Well, who cares? You look absolutely darling no matter what. Now run along and get
yourself dried off and we'll get this party organized.
The birthday girl's not to do a thing, anyway."

Jenny stopped long enough to pick up the planter
and escaped, taking the fern with her into the bedroom. She put it on the bureau and then sank onto the
edge of the bed in complete misery. She reached up for
the towel, which had turned wet and clammy, pulled it
off her hair and let the strands hang limply. She would
have to call Ben. But the telephone was in the living
room, and how could she explain this awful thing that
had happened with the others right there? Still, she had

to do it. Even with no one listening it would be painful enough, trying to make him understand.... No, that wasn't it. He'd understand quickly enough. But how could she make him see that it wasn't something she wanted? How could she let him know—

There was a knock at the bedroom door, and Philip's voice.

"Jenny dear, now don't rush, but could you tell me where I can find a dish—you know, a big bowl or something—to put the ceviche in."

"Shelf over the counter—left of the sink," she replied, doing her best to keep her voice normal and adding, "be right out."

His footsteps retreated, and Jenny tried to take herself in hand, hurrying to brush her hair and give it a quick pass with the dryer. Then, keeping her eyes firmly away from the green dress, she pulled on jeans and a sweatshirt—her usual outfit—and a pair of moccasins.

As she opened the door to go back out she could hear Philip saying confidentially, "Well, of course you know what a legend Buzz Carmichael is. A law unto himself. And doesn't this place just look it? Marvelous, isn't it? It's a pretty big plum to be invited here by the old man, so the talk goes in Boston." He turned at Jenny's approach. "Ah, there she is. I was just telling Craig about the place."

"Yes. Philip, will you excuse me for a minute? I have to make a quick phone call."

"Well, phone away, darling. And then let's have some champagne, for heaven's sake."

Jenny glanced at her watch nervously and started for the telephone when there was a knock at the back door. Tina, who was still puttering in the kitchen, opened it before Jenny could move.

"Welcome, whoever you are," Tina sang out. "The party's just about to start, so come on in."

"Excuse me, I didn't realize..." she heard Ben say, but the exuberant Tina was pulling him inside.

Jenny was sure her heart stopped beating for a second. He had changed into khaki pants and a fresh blue shirt. His thick black hair glistened with moisture from the shower. Dark blue eyes went around the group quickly, pausing when they came to Jenny, who was standing still, unable to move.

"Well, hi there," Philip said cordially. "Let's see now, it's Ben, isn't it? Ben..."

"Sullivan," he supplied.

"Yes, of course. Well, come on in, Ben. The party's just about to start. It's Jenny's birthday. This is Craig Downing, and the lively lady who let you in is Tina Beckwith. Ben takes care of the summer places up here, and Jenny tells me he's been very helpful with Chris," he explained to Craig. "Where is Chris, by the way?"

"He's with friends," Jenny said. "And Philip, I should explain, Ben isn't just..." She paused helplessly and cast a pleading look at Ben. "Philip and Craig and Tina surprised me just now, Ben."

"So I see." His voice was pleasant and even, but Jenny could see that his jaw was clenched, making the faint indentation in his chin show up more.

Philip went on, horribly unstoppable, pulling an envelope out of his pocket and waving it above his head.

"Cause for celebration here," he announced. "I mean, in addition to the birthday, of course." He pulled Jenny into a hug. "I stopped by your place to check your mail, Jenny. Now I haven't steamed this

open, darling, I swear, but I know what's in it. I had
lunch with Will Forrester—the dean of the law
school," he explained to Ben, whose head dipped
slightly in acknowledgment. "And he let me in on the
secret. This girl not only passed her contract-law exam
but placed first in the class."

Tina let out a small squeal, and she and Craig duti-
fully applauded.

Ben's eyes were on Jenny's face. She could feel them
burning straight through her.

"Congratulations," he said quietly.

Philip continued, "Now that's cause enough for re-
joicing, I'd say, but what I'm really hoping is that this
is the weekend I talk her into announcing our engagement." He kept his arm around her waist, not allow-
ing her the chance to get away. "Craig, why don't we
break open that champagne and get this party started?
Join us, won't you, Ben? We've brought all kinds of
good stuff from Boston. The more the merrier."

"Oh, yes, do," Tina bubbled, seizing him by the arm
and looking earnestly into his face. "We've brought
ceviche from Bellisario's. I know you'll love it. Ceviche
is this dish where they blanch the shrimp and scallops
and then they add all this good stuff—scallions and red
pepper and avocado and a whole lot of other things."

Ben looked down at her kindly, detaching himself
from her grasp. "Very nice of you," he said evenly. "It
sounds delicious. But I've already made dinner plans.
Congratulations again, Jenny. For everything." He
retreated quickly through the kitchen door, and the
sound of his truck driving away echoed through Jenny's head.

Philip turned to her. "I think this girl's still in
shock," he said heartily. "But we'll fix that. Here,

open your letter and read the good news yourself. The rest of us will bring out the goodies. Craig, how about that champagne?"

"Coming right up."

"I wish he'd stayed," Tina said. "He seemed like a very nice fellow, that Ben."

Craig shot her a resentful look as he headed for the kitchen.

While the rest of them bustled about bringing glasses, opening the wine and then digging into hampers for the food they'd brought, Jenny turned the envelope over in her hands. Only three weeks ago this would have caused her the wildest joy. Now, when she opened it, the words ran together, jumbled and meaningless.

Philip handed her a glass, and she sipped at the champagne and tried to smile. It had a dry, sour taste, and all she could think of was the sweet outdoor tang of the food Ben had cooked for them only hours before and how they'd sat on the ground looking at the water as they ate.

She got through the dinner somehow, nodding and smiling when a remark was addressed to her. Craig and Tina, as if determined to keep the party at a high pitch of excitement, talked nonstop, and even Philip, who was drinking more champagne than Jenny had ever seen him drink before, grew garrulous and confiding.

"The way I see it, honey, what we ought to do when you get back to Boston is make a tiny bit more of an effort to reconcile with your dad. You've made a good start, asking him about borrowing this place. And wasn't he just as willing and welcoming as you could've wanted? Now that's a beginning." He turned to the others. "Family misunderstandings," he explained with an air of mystery. "You know how they are. But nothing that can't be straightened out."

Jenny drew a painful breath and said nothing.

"Do us a lot of good in our profession," he went on, pouring himself more wine. "Man like Buzz Carmichael—"

Tina let out a little shriek. "Oh, is *he* your dad? I've heard of him. Gosh, I guess everybody has. Like Melvin Belli."

Jenny grimaced and looked down at her plate, shoving the expensive restaurant food around with her fork. It tasted like sawdust to her.

It was ten o'clock before Craig and Tina left for the motel where they'd made reservations. Jenny lingered in the kitchen for a few minutes after seeing them off, putting away food and stacking dishes as Philip wandered back into the living room where a fire had been lighted as the evening turned cool. When Jenny rejoined him, she found him slumped in a chair, sound asleep. The long drive and an unaccustomed amount of champagne had done their work, she guessed. She went over to him and shook him gently.

"I'm awfully tired, Philip," she said. "Let's turn in, shall we? I'll get a flashlight for you. Your room's all made up in the guest house."

"Oh." He woke up, looking startled and then momentarily disappointed. He sighed and pulled himself up out of the chair, took the flashlight from her and kissed her good-night before making his stumbling way down the path to the guest house.

Jenny waited a few minutes, until the lights in his bedroom went out. Then she pulled on a heavy black-and-red shirt, which was hanging by the back door, found another flashlight and went out of the house, hurrying quickly and quietly toward Ben's house.

The temperature had taken its normal plunge, and Jenny shivered as she hurried along the dirt road. Her moccasins were poor protection against stones and ruts. Something hot and choking burned in her throat, and she had to fight to keep the tears from starting up.

His windows were closed against the chilly air, but she could see lights in the living room. She paused in front of the door, feeling a heavy weight of anxiety in her stomach. Then she lifted her hand and knocked.

He had changed into what looked like well-worn corduroys and an old blue pullover. In the dim light she scanned his features with a kind of desperation, and a small catch came into her voice when she tried to speak.

"Ben, I—"

"You know, you have a way of dropping in at the oddest times."

There was amusement in the words, but it sounded brittle somehow, with none of the soft intimacy she had heard earlier in the day.

"I wanted to explain..."

"There's nothing to explain, is there? Things seem perfectly clear to me." He turned to go back into the living room, and she followed, closing the door behind her.

"But I didn't know they were coming. I don't see how it's my fault."

"I'm not blaming you." They stood facing each other in front of the low-burning fire.

"But I feel so awful!" she burst out. "It was such a perfect day, and then it was all spoiled."

His mouth moved in a one-sided smile. "Oh, not totally spoiled. I called Jed Benton, an old fishing buddy of mine, and we both went to Mrs. McCracken's. Sensational crabs. Not Bellisario's, of course."

"That's not fair."

The half smile faded. "No, it isn't. I shouldn't have said it." But he kept his distance, not asking her to sit, not making a move to touch her. "Anyway, if you consider your birthday spoiled by your future husband showing up unexpectedly..." He let the sentence hang in the air.

"He's not my future husband!" Jenny retorted. She stopped, red and confused.

"Oh, really? He seems to think he is." Ben's tone was bitter now. "Seems to me I heard an engagement mentioned."

"Philip and I have things to talk over and decide. There is a lot we have to settle."

He stepped back, putting more distance between them. Beside them the coffee table held a rumpled newspaper that had been tossed down carelessly. He must have been reading it when she knocked.

"It's a little hard to make decisions when you don't know what you want," he said with infuriating calmness.

"I do know what I want!"

He gave her a probing look and moved closer to the fireplace, propping one elbow on the mantel. He had stood that way the last time she was here, she recalled. And that time he had kissed her. The remembrance of it swept over her with sudden pain. Tonight was different, she could tell.

"You think you know," he said slowly. "And today—well, up until this evening, I thought I knew what you wanted, too."

"But you're blaming me for all of it! I had nothing to do with those people coming here."

He said, still patiently, "This is not about those people coming here, Jenny. It's about you making decisions."

Red waves of anger began to sweep over Jenny. She could feel her fists clenching at her sides.

"Don't you dare lecture me about making decisions," she said in an icy voice. "I've been doing just that for twelve years, and I've done it all alone. There was never anybody to help me. I've brought up Chris, I've worked, I've gone to college, and every single thing I've decided by myself."

He studied her for a moment. "Yes, I'm sure you have," he said in a quiet voice. "I don't mean to belittle what you've done. But that's what life's about, Jenny. Making decisions. Over and over again. It never stops."

"Well, then that's one thing I know how to do," she flared. "I've had plenty of practice. And I think I can keep on doing it without any help from you, Judge Sullivan."

Without waiting for him to answer, she whirled around and strode out into the night.

CRAIG AND TINA appeared late the next morning, and Jenny, who had spent an all but sleepless night, struggled to maintain cordiality as she went about the kitchen looking for ingredients to make up a brunch for all of them before they started back to Boston. She could hardly wait for them to be gone, for the house to be quiet again. Philip, somewhat subdued after the unaccustomed celebrating of the night before, said the bacon smelled wonderful, but what he really needed right now was some of that wonderful espresso from Bellisario's. Too bad they hadn't been able to include that in one of the hampers. He and Craig both laughed, but then assured her that the peaceful ambience at Tucker's Pond made up for any slight inconvenience.

"Like being out of reach of Bellisario's for a whole day?" Jenny snapped, and both of them looked at her, startled, before continuing with their conversation. Tina was fretting over a broken fingernail.

"I've been letting them grow, see," she explained after Jenny had produced an emery board. "Now I have to decide whether to file them all back and start over. Of course I could just let this one catch up."

"That might be best," Jenny agreed, biting her tongue to keep from making any more ill-tempered remarks.

They were just sitting down to eat when Chris came in. He cast a look around the table, so obviously disappointed that Jenny rallied quickly to say, "Lots of surprise company, isn't that fun, Chris? Did you have a good time at the Hazeltons'? This is Mr. Downing and that's Miss Beckwith. You know Philip, of course."

"Hi, sport," Philip said heartily. "How's the vacation going? Been doing lots of fishing, I'll bet."

"Some," Chris said.

"Catching a lot?" Craig asked.

"A few."

"I've always thought I'd like fishing," Tina said brightly. "Only I wouldn't like digging up all those worms."

Chris sent a withering look in her direction.

"I don't use worms," he said. "I use flies."

"Oh, my word. They must be terribly hard to catch."

Jenny held her breath, hoping Chris wouldn't retort rudely, but Philip stepped into the breach, laughing.

"I can see you need a short course in fly-fishing, Tina. We'll explain it to you on the way home." He turned back to Chris. "Some tan. Looks as if you've been outdoors often enough."

"Yeah."

"Well! How about something to eat, Chris?" Jenny asked hastily. One part of her was mortified at the boy's curtness, but the other part, she had to admit, didn't blame him. When people made such absolutely senseless remarks, how else should you act?

"Mrs. Hazelton made us a big breakfast," he answered. "I'm not hungry." Then he went to his room without another word.

"Oh, isn't he a sweetie?" Tina bubbled. "You certainly are lucky to have a great kid like that."

"I know I am," Jenny said, looking at the closed door and feeling suddenly light-years away from all of them around the table.

"Fine boy," Philip chimed in. "Needs a bit of firmness and guidance occasionally, but that's easily taken care of."

She saw them off at about one, Tina declaring expansively that she felt absolutely renewed. "All this marvelous fresh air! You know, we should do this on a regular basis—it does simply wonderful things for the psyche."

Philip agreed, but added that he hoped Jenny had had enough renewal by now. "Can't wait for you to get back to Boston, darling. I meant what I said last night about that engagement. Hurry home so we can start making plans."

She couldn't tell him, any more than she'd been able to tell him anything all weekend with the others hovering so close, that Boston seemed like another planet, and that this place was starting to feel more like home than the city ever had. "Thank you all for coming," she called after them, waving. Then she turned back into the house, moving slowly and without spirit.

There was no sound from Chris's room, and she guessed that he was sprawled on his bed, absorbed in the book that was never far away from him now. She thought of going to him, but decided against it. She felt too tired, too confused, too vulnerable herself to deal with what she knew was troubling him. The things that were troubling her would have to be dealt with first.

She tidied the kitchen before getting out the broom and sweeping. She moved into the main room and began straightening and dusting, then went to her bedroom and did the same. She brought the fern and planter out and placed them in a sunny window, lingering for a moment and touching the soft green fronds with the tip of one finger, remembering Ben's smile when he'd brought it to her and how he'd bent to kiss her softly on the cheek.

Was it possible that she'd been working, planning, expending all her energy these past few years in pursuit of a life that no longer meant anything to her? She thought back to that first morning after their arrival.

She'd gone to Ben's house with her coffee mug in hand and they'd talked at his kitchen table. She'd told him about her plans, about hoping to pass the bar and be admitted to the firm, and he'd answered in that lazy, half-mocking way, ''And then your daddy will realize that you really do amount to something.''

It had made her angry to hear his easy flippancy, but had there been a grain of truth in it? Had much of her life been made up of acts of defiance against her father? Jenny shook her head impatiently. No, there was more to it. She loved the law and her study of it. She truly did want to become a lawyer. She and Philip had spent hours talking about their plans for the future, about what they would accomplish together. Why, then, was it suddenly all coming apart at the seams?

Jenny sat on the worn couch, picked up a cushion and hugged it to her as she looked toward the lake. It was coming apart because of a pair of the darkest blue eyes she had ever seen. Because of a crooked smile and a mouth that set her whole body on fire when it was pressed against her own. Because of strong hands that moved over her back, holding her so close she became breathless. She had dreamed about those hands at night, lying alone in her bed.

Philip was a good man and kind in his way. Ambitious, of course, but she'd never minded that. And if her being Buzz Carmichael's daughter had been part of what he admired about her, well, who was she to criticize motives? For hadn't she seen in him a refuge, a home for her and Chris? If only she could feel with him a tiny bit of the spark that ignited in her when she was in Ben's arms. But was that really important? Should the decisions of a lifetime hinge upon a kiss, a voice and a pair of broad shoulders? Jenny closed her eyes and leaned back. A small throbbing had started in her temples.

She heard the sound of a door opening and glanced toward it. Chris was standing there watching her.

"Do we really have to go back?" he asked. She could see the worried, faraway look in his eyes.

She raised her eyebrows and sat up straighter.

"I mean to Boston," he said, pressing on. "Do we have to go back there to live?"

"You know we do, Chris."

"Why? Some people live here all year round. Ben does. Couldn't we do that?"

"I'm getting my degree this year, Chris. You know I have to go back to finish up my studies."

"Yeah, okay. But you'll be done in January, you said so. What about after that?" His eyes pleaded with her.

"Look, Chris, this isn't our house. It's your grandfather's house."

"Most of the time it's just empty."

"Even so, it's his, not ours. And it's a summer place. It's not built for winter."

"We could fix it up for winter. Ben knows how."

"There are other reasons. My job, for one thing. I have to work, you know that, Chris. And where would you go to school?"

"They have schools in Maine!"

"Yes, of course they do, but…Chris, I thought you understood how things are. All my contacts are in Boston, the people I know in the profession. There wouldn't be anything for me to do here, don't you see?"

"Ben's a lawyer and he lives here," he said stubbornly.

Jenny took a deep breath, casting about for an explanation and finding none. Was it because she was trying to explain it to herself at the same time? Chris said nothing for a few seconds, simply stood there regarding her in a frank, studying way. At last he said, "So I guess you're going to marry Philip, after all, right?" It seemed to Jenny that he was figuring out something in his mind, getting all the facts straight.

She could feel a flush in her cheeks. She hesitated and then said carefully, "Philip wants us with him. We'd be a family, live in a house, do things together."

Chris's stare was so direct it made Jenny uncomfortable.

"Big deal," the boy said finally.

"Now Chris, that's not fair," she said.

"Well, this is where I want to live," he said, and there was a slight tremble in his voice. "If I can't do it now, I'll do it later, as soon as I can leave school. I'll come up here and build myself a house. Ben's grandfather tells how in the book. I know I could do it."

"Oh, Chris, I wish it were that easy," Jenny said, her breath rushing out in a sigh. "I know it all looks simple to you, but believe me, it isn't. There are so many things to be thought through. Most of all I have to finish law school, get my degree, then take the bar exams. You know that—I was sure you understood."

"Yeah, I know all that stuff." He was looking at the floor now, not meeting her eyes.

"Chris, I only want what's best for us—for you especially." She stopped uncertainly, remembering Philip thought that Chris needed a good boarding school. The pounding in her head grew stronger. "We'll talk about this some more later," she promised.

He raised his eyes and gave her a long steady look, then turned and went outside. She watched through the window as he walked, hands in his pockets, down toward the dock. When he reached it, he stood gazing out over the water for a time. Finally he turned to find a stone and hurled it, skimming and whistling, out over the lake.

That night when she went to bed she raised her window in spite of the evening chill, then crawled under the covers and lay in a huddle of misery. Softly, and from far away, she heard faint strains of music.

CHAPTER NINE

CHRIS WAS QUIET the next day, not renewing the discussion, and Jenny, although she was relieved, still harbored a faint uneasiness. Their talk had been inconclusive. Nothing really satisfying had come out of it for either of them. She took the now familiar walk along the dirt road to the mailbox, finding only advertising circulars. It was a bright brisk day and she lingered on her way back, looking at the thick growth of ferns under the trees that lined the road on both sides. In one place was a wide sweep of glossy-leaved myrtle. Surely that hadn't grown wild here, Jenny thought. Someone had probably set out a couple of plants once. Maybe even her own mother. She remembered wistfully how she had walked this way with her mother long ago.

Her feet slowed as she thought about how many years had passed and how many years she'd been alone with no one to confide in. She shook her head to clear it and went on walking. It wouldn't have made a difference. There would have been the same problems and responsibilities. And eventually she would have had to face them alone. No wonder she'd felt it such an unfair blow when Ben had accused her of waffling. At the thought of him, of the way he'd looked the last time she'd seen him, the warm fires of longing began to curl inside her, like new flames licking around a log. She'd dated over the years, of course, but somehow she'd always been too tired or distracted or worried about the sitter she'd engaged for Chris to enjoy herself. And in the end she'd wound up putting more and more distance between herself and the men who might have been interested in her. Until Philip, of course, whom she'd met when she went to work for Prescott, Turner and Bowing. And they had drifted into a love affair based more on convenience than passion, it sometimes seemed to her. Although perhaps the passion was there—on Philip's side, anyway. Her own feelings in that regard were much as they'd always been. She'd felt warmth and friendship for Philip, but little beyond that. She'd never awakened in the night wanting his head to be on the pillow beside her or feeling that she could hardly wait for the day to begin so she might see him again.

As she did with Ben.

But there were worlds of difference between her and Ben. Chiefly his obvious disapproval of the way she was managing her life. And the last time they talked he had been critical, overbearing. Anger sent color into her cheeks as she thought of it, and she started walking faster. He'd accused her of weakness, indecisiveness. He was totally unsympathetic to the problems she faced. She stopped short in the middle of the narrow dirt road. He was also gentle and unfailingly kind to a troubled boy. He'd brought a green growing plant for her birthday, and his strong hands had almost spanned her waist when he'd lifted her over a fallen tree in the path. And his lips, tracing her own, then encompassing them, had spoken wordlessly of a desire that Jenny had answered with her own. These nights she woke wishing with all her heart that he was there with her.

She started walking again slowly. She had promised to marry Philip.

Chris was out when she got back to the house. She supposed he was exploring the woods and paths, something he never seemed to tire of. She went into her bedroom and got out the bundle of legal papers that she'd brought with her and that she'd scarcely glanced at since her arrival. She carried them into the living room and began going over them, trying to refresh her memory about all these matters that had once seemed so important. How trivial it all seemed now, she thought with some wonder. Wrangling and comflicting claims, opposing points of view, legal technicalities. She ran her fingers through her hair, got up and made fresh coffee and tackled them again, making marginal notes in pencil.

Ben Sullivan's face kept getting between her and the words. His voice, level and reasonable on the surface yet steely underneath, held a sureness Jenny longed to feel herself. How could one ever be that sure? That was what life was, he'd told her. Making decisions, over and over. It never stopped. And more than his words was the touch, taste and nearness of him. Jenny could close her eyes and imagine the strength of his arms around her, the warmth of his mouth on hers. She could lose herself in the blue depths of his eyes.

She stood up suddenly, upsetting her papers. Her pencil went flying across the room and her hands came up to press against both sides of her face. More than she had ever wanted anything, she wanted to run to him now, to forget about all decisions and find a haven in his arms. But she sensed she had done too many things wrong, hurt him in ways she'd never intended. And how could she turn her back on the goals she was so close to achieving after all the years of work and self-denial?

She knelt down and began picking up the papers, piling them helter-skelter and trying to hold back the tears that were turning the room misty.

By midafternoon Chris had still not returned, not even for lunch. Very likely he had taken a sandwich with him, Jenny thought. She made one for herself and did her best to eat it. The day, which had started out so fine, had clouded over and turned blustery, with a strong wind blowing from the north that was causing the temperature to drop rapidly. It felt more like November than July, Jenny thought, yet she was too familiar with Maine's unpredictable weather to think twice about it. Still, if Chris had gone out wearing only a T-shirt and jeans he'd be chilled through before he got home. She went to the back door and looked out. There was no sign of him. She walked around to the front of the house and glanced down at the dock. The canoe was in place, securely tied. She was glad he wasn't on the lake, at least, for she could see white-caps forming under the strong wind. Still, she felt anxious as she went back into the house.

She hesitated only briefly, then went to the telephone and called Adele Hazelton.

"Oh, hello, Jenny." Adele's voice was cheerful, a shaft of warmth in the cold. "Isn't this weather just turning around on us? I meant to call you about the blueberries—they're ripening fast. If you and Chris want some, come over any time. Bring your own buckets, though."

"Thanks, Adele. We'd love to. Uh, the reason I'm calling is to see if Chris is over there."

"Here?"

"Yes, he's been gone for quite a while and I can't imagine where he is."

There was a pause, a small silence over the wire, and Jenny knew the other woman was thinking about the rainy night when Chris had run off. Then Adele said heartily, "Oh, my goodness, I'm sure he's just lost track of time. In fact, why don't you call Ben? He might've stopped over there."

"Yes, that's a good idea. I'll do that. Thanks, Adele."

It was what Jenny had been thinking herself, she realized as she put down the phone. Where else could he be? But she still dreaded calling Ben. Finally she picked up the telephone again and dialed Ben's number. She waited and waited. No answer. She hung up and sat quietly. It was still quite possible that Chris was with Ben. They might have gone anywhere together, perhaps on an errand in the pickup, perhaps just into the yard to split wood for the fireplace or mend a fence.

She took a deep breath and told herself not to panic. She was being irrationally concerned. She'd wait awhile, and then if he hadn't returned for supper, she'd walk over to Ben's and see for herself. But surely she wouldn't have to. Chris was bound to be back in time to eat.

Six o'clock came and went. The dark cloud cover seemed to thicken and the twilight to move in with alarming speed. Jenny called Ben's house again. Still no answer. Chris couldn't be with Ben, she told herself. He would never let Chris stay away this long without telephoning. He would know she'd worry.

She went outside and walked around the immediate area. She made her way to the guest house and looked in both rooms. She even peered into the little pump house. Finally she cupped her hands to her mouth and called his name. The wind whipped the sound away. She was shivering when she went back into the house. She went around closing all the windows, turning on lights. How long should she wait before doing something? And what should she do? Call the police? She remembered one name, Officer Berton. Perhaps she could reach him.

She stood in the middle of the living room, hugging herself to control the trembling that was only partly caused by the cold. And then suddenly it came to her. She knew where Chris was. She let her breath out in a sudden gasp as the realization hit her. Of course. The one place that he would see as a refuge, the one place that had captivated him. The little fishing cabin they'd gone to on her birthday. But what had happened to him? Why hadn't he come back when it had started to get dark? She remembered how rough and overgrown the path was—Ben had said it should be cleared with a chain saw. It would be easy to lose your way at dusk. And suppose Chris was out there now in the cold, plunging around in the woods, lost and frightened?

Jenny dashed to the back door and opened it. Then she paused and forced herself to think logically. She would be no good to Chris if she went tearing off unprepared. She closed the door and hurried to the bedroom, where she changed from her moccasins into sturdy running shoes. Then she put on a heavy sweater and tied an extra one for Chris around her waist so that her hands would be free. Last of all she found a flashlight. Then she started out, the wind catching at her as she pulled the door shut behind her.

She was pretty sure she could find the path to the cabin, only it had been daylight that other time. Everything looked different at night. When she came to the fork in the road she peered to the left, trying to see if there were lights on at Ben's house. She would have given anything for his strength and his knowledge of the woods right now. But his place was dark. Jenny looked around carefully until she spotted the path, then took a deep breath and plunged through the thick trees.

She found her way well enough at first, casting her flashlight beam around in a wide arc as she went. Once in a while she called out his name, but the only answer was the high wail of the wind as it bent the tops of the trees above her head. The farther she walked, the more difficult maintaining her footing became. Her anxiety was increasing, as well, along with the certainly that this was indeed where Chris had gone. But he'd been away all day, she thought worriedly. If he'd started back late in the afternoon, he might have been floundering around in the dark for hours. She tried to put such thoughts out of her head and concentrate on the path before her.

Fear for Chris's safety translated itself into anger as she struggled over encroaching roots and fallen trees. She thought he'd learned an important lesson after the episode with the car. She'd been so sure he'd never try this sort of foolish thing again. Hadn't he gotten the message that running away from a problem was no solution? Maybe Philip was right in thinking that greater discipline was what he needed. Maybe sending him away to school wasn't the worst idea in the world. Had all the changes she thought she'd seen in Chris been only wishful thinking? When they returned to Boston, were the same old problems going to surface again? The silence, the moodiness, the rebelliousness—

A thunderous cracking sounded above her. Jenny
froze as a huge dead limb broke from a tree and
crashed across the path almost directly in front of her.
For a moment she was unable to move, and her mouth
was dry with fear. Cautiously she left the path and
made her way around the obstacle, grabbing branches
along the way for support and at last finding her feet
on more even ground. She held tightly to her flashlight and crept forward until she came to the big fallen
tree trunk that Ben had lifted her over. She closed her
eyes briefly against the sudden pain of that memory
and scrambled over the trunk with some difficulty,
scraping one hand as she did so but scarcely noticing.
Anxiously she hurried forward, her sense of urgency
growing stronger and stronger.

To her left the land fell away into a shallow ravine
that she also remembered from the day of the picnic.
She had stopped to look at it then, admiring the beauty
of the verdant ferns, which grew in such profusion
down to the tiny stream trickling through the woods.
Nervously she kept her eye on the slope, not wanting
to lose her footing and tumble down it. How long had
she been gone? Minutes? Hours? She had no idea.

She thought she must be getting closer to the little
cabin and began to call out and scan the woods on either side of her more intently. But then, as she peered
along the shaft of light cast by her flashlight, her toe
caught on a root in the path and she went sprawling.
The flashlight flew from her hand, and she felt a sharp
pain in her knee. She lay motionless till her breath
came back, and in a moment she was able to sit up and
realize she wasn't badly hurt. She felt her knee where
the denim of her jeans had torn and guessed there was
some bleeding, but not a serious amount. *Be careful,*

she scolded herself. Then she began searching for the flashlight. Crouching close to the ground she tried feeling for it with her outstretched hands, concentrating so hard that she didn't hear another ominous cracking sound above her. So she had no warning that a heavy branch was crashing toward her until it struck, sending her tumbling over and over into the ferny ravine.

WHEREVER SHE WAS, she thought dimly, it was dark as a pocket. But that was all right, because she would simply sleep here until the sun came up. The only problem was that rain was coming in somewhere. A leaky roof, that was it. But Ben could fix it. He knew about things like that. All at once everything seemed so simple. She recalled that she had been troubled and confused only a short time ago. Whatever for? What was there to be confused about? She was in love with Ben—that was all there was to it. And things would be fine now that she realized it. She squinted slightly against a sudden pain in her head. What she'd better do, she thought, was sleep for a little while until the pain went away. By that time she'd feel like sitting up and she would talk it all over with Ben. . . .

The next time she awoke she was shivering. Her head was pounding and reality washed over her with desperate clarity. She was hurt, and no one knew where she was. She and Ben were hardly even friends; she'd pushed him away with her silly vacillating. She'd been stupid enough to think she might be able to marry Philip even though it was Ben she loved. The only man she'd ever loved, she realized. Now it was all too late. And Chris—she struggled to move but could only moan and fall back—Chris was lost somewhere in the woods. Distantly she could hear the wailing of the wind, and blackness closed over her again.

It was still dark when she came to a third time, but now something had changed. She was no longer lying on the ground. Strong arms were around her and she could feel a rough material against her cheek. Someone was holding her...carrying her. She tried to speak.

"Ben?" But there was no answer, and she was not sure she'd managed to make her voice work. She drifted in and out of consciousness. First there was only the blackness, but then lights appeared, and once she saw a face bending over her, taut with worry, dark blue eyes scanning her features. She tried to lift her hand to touch him, wanting to smooth away the worry lines, wanting to let him know she was all right. But her limbs were cold and heavy as lead, and no matter how she tried to keep her eyes open, they shut again, as a blessed warmth stole over her.

Later she awoke to see that she was indoors, well bundled in blankets and lying close to a cheerful fire. Ben was wringing out a cloth and placing it on her forehead.

"Ben..." This time she managed to make him hear her. His whole face seemed to collapse with relief as he looked down at her.

"Jenny." Just her name, nothing more, and she quickly said, "Chris. We have to find Chris. He's—"

"I'm right here, Mom." Painfully, she moved her head to the right and saw him sitting beside her with Blaze.

She put out her hand and he seized it.

"Gosh, I didn't know anybody was worried about me," he said, and Jenny, with relief flooding over her and tears threatening, wasn't sure whether to laugh or cry.

"Oh, Chris," she said helplessly. "I thought...I thought there wasn't going to be any more running away."

He looked surprised. "Heck, Mom, I wasn't running away. I just had some thinking to do. Ben said nobody could do it for me, and I thought the cabin would be a real good place so that's why I came here."

Jenny looked around and realized for the first time that this was indeed the cabin and that she was lying on a narrow cot drawn up to the fire. "But...what happened?" she asked, her gaze swinging back to Ben. He was still watching her as if memorizing her face.

"I guess one of those tall pines had it in for you." He smiled. "When I found you, you were lying in the gully with your feet in the water."

Jenny moved her toes. They were snug and warm in heavy socks now. "How did you know where to look? I called your house, but no one answered."

"I'd gone to my office in town to look over the mail and see if anything needed attention. Later I stopped at Adele's and she mentioned that you were looking for Chris. So I thought of the cabin. I wasn't worried about Chris, though."

"You weren't?" In spite of the pain in her head, Jenny thought she'd never felt so comfortable, so secure and happy. Ben was near, Chris was okay, and the fire was making snug crackling sounds that shut out the wind's howl.

"No, because Blaze was missing, too, and I figured he was with Chris. I was pretty sure no serious harm would come to him as long as he had Blaze with him."

"One time I did get a little bit lost," Chris admitted. "But Blaze knew the way. I meant to come home earlier," he added sheepishly. "What happened was, I made a fire and then me and Blaze sort of . . . well, we fell asleep."

Like babes in the woods, Jenny thought, and the rush of tenderness she felt for him drove out anger. She squeezed his hand. "Just don't do it again, buster," she said.

She looked at Ben, but he had walked away and was gazing out one of the cabin's small front windows. When he turned back moments later, Jenny felt her heart go cold, even though the rest of her was comfortably warm. His expression, which had been full of love and concern only a short time before, had changed. He avoided her eyes and seemed far away, a stranger with no interest in her beyond seeing that she was safe.

Some of the thoughts that had run through her head when she'd lain in the ravine came back to her now. She had seen it clearly then—the way her feelings for Ben had made it impossible for her to consider marrying Philip. How could she when all her thoughts were on Ben? When the memory of his touch sent flames running through her body? But Ben's distant look now told her exactly what he thought of her. He considered her an ambitious, hard-hearted woman with a calculating eye to the future, one who would never allow a little thing like love to change her carefully laid plans.

She longed to cry out to him, to try to explain. But his austere bearing stopped her. She could tell anything to the Ben who had gazed at her with such love and concern moments ago. But this was a man with a look of dark, forbidding privacy. Someone she scarcely knew. His next words only confirmed her thoughts.

"I don't think we should try to make it back tonight," he said curtly. "That wind isn't dying down any, and it could be dangerous. We'll wait till morning. Chris, there's a sleeping bag in the corner—you can take that. You're comfortable where you are?" he asked Jenny, but didn't use her name, she noticed.

"I'm fine," she said in a small voice. "What about you?"

"I'll be okay in the chair here," he said.

Jenny didn't dare offer an argument.

Chris gave her a good-night kiss, which she couldn't remember him doing for years, and lingered for a moment, as if making sure she was really all right. Then he climbed into the sleeping bag and fell asleep almost at once with Blaze curled up close to him. Ben sank into a wooden chair with a sloping back and faded cushions and closed his eyes. The fire burned steadily but more quietly now, the only light in the cabin.

Jenny tried to sleep, but every part of her seemed to throb with pain, and not all of it, she thought, was from her injuries. Glancing at her sleeping son and then glancing more cautiously at Ben, she was able to pretend for a brief moment that they were a family. That was what they looked like—a real family having an adventure they would remember and talk about for years. They would laugh about it, secure in their love for one another....

But then cold reality stole in, shattering the picture. They weren't a family, and they never would be. Everything had slipped away. They had missed the crucial moment when it might have all come together. *She* had missed it. Tears burned in her eyes and trickled down both sides of her face, and it was a long time before she fell into fitful sleep.

Once in the night, with the fire burning low and the wind still keening, she awoke and opened her eyes, but at once closed them again, for Ben was beside her and even without looking, she could feel him studying her. He stood over her for several minutes before throwing another log onto the fire and returning to his chair.

They left at first daylight, and even though Jenny insisted she could walk, Ben shook his head in a way that brooked no argument and carried her. The wind had died down and the day showed the innocent face of summer, denying the fury of the storm the night before. Only the debris strewn across the path remained as a reminder. Once when he was obliged to put her down to negotiate an obstacle, Jenny felt a sharp pain in her knee, and guessed that she'd wrenched it when she'd fallen. He must have seen the spasm that crossed her face but said nothing, only picked her up again and walked on. She felt the rough wool of his shirt against her cheek, the strong steady beat of his heart beneath it. She thought he had never been so close to her—or so far away.

Adele came to visit that afternoon, clanging up to the back door and letting herself in, yoo-hooing as she entered. Chris had gone off at last after sticking so close all day that Jenny finally suggested he might like to take out the canoe and paddle as far as the osprey's nest. The day was sunny and serene, and she was sitting stretched out on the porch with her feet on a stool.

"Brought you some supper," Adele called from inside. "Now, don't get up. I'll just put it here on the table."

Jenny heard the clink of dishes, and then Adele joined her on the porch. She was wearing worn jeans and a sweatshirt that read Tucker's Pond Tigers. Her wiry gray hair stuck out every which way.

"Well! I'll just bet everything aches today," she said cheerfully, sitting down on the other chair.

"Adele, you're wonderful. Thanks so much for the food. I do feel a little stiff, but that's all. And there's a dandy lump on my head." Jenny felt it gingerly with her fingertips.

"I heard. Talked to Ben this morning. We were all worried to death about you and Chris with that wind last night. How's the knee?"

"A little gimpy," Jenny said. "Nothing that won't be all right in a day or two."

Adele shook her head. "Kids. Aren't they the limit? But that Chris is a smart one. I was sure he'd be fine. He and my grandson Bud got along so well the other night you'd've thought they were lifelong pals."

"I'm afraid I misjudged him," Jenny admitted. "I thought he'd run away again." Adele nodded sympathetically, and Jenny went on more slowly, "I guess I've been doing a lot of that lately. Getting everything wrong, I mean."

Adele looked out over the lake. "Oh well, it's easy to misjudge the ones who mean the most to us, isn't it? I've done it myself, more times than I care to count."

Jenny gave a wry smile. "I don't believe it. Not you. You seem to see everything so clearly." She gave a little shake of her head. "I don't know what's the matter with me lately. I always thought I knew what I wanted, what kind of life. But up here... I think there must be something about this place. It makes you see things differently. Now I'm not so sure what I'm doing is right—for me or for Chris."

Adele looked at her kindly. "You'll be back in Boston soon. Maybe it'll all look different to you then."

"It already looks different to Chris," Jenny said with a weak smile. "He wants to come back here and build himself a house in the woods."

"Isn't that funny? That's just the kind of kid Ben Sullivan was. Of course we used to only see him summers, but still, you could tell. It seems as if it's worked out all right for him."

"Chris likes Ben a lot. Ben's really made a difference to him."

Adele glanced at Jenny and seemed about to say something, then shook her head. "You're a smart girl, Jenny," she said briskly. "I think you do the right thing more often than you realize. Don't you worry about it."

If my mother were alive, Jenny thought with a pang, *she'd have said things like that. We'd have talked together this way....*

"You've been such a good friend, Adele," she said, and Adele's eyes blinked rapidly as she leaned over to pat Jenny's hand.

Adele came back the next day with more food, but on the third day Jenny insisted she was much improved and could manage for herself. She even demonstrated, walking across the floor with scarcely a limp.

"Well, I'm glad I was able to help some," Adele said. "After this week I'll be going back to work. Court will be back in business, and of course I act as Ben's legal secretary, too."

Jenny had guessed as much. "And we'll be heading home to Boston," she said wistfully.

"Yes, I suppose so, but mercy, you'll be back. I know that well enough. Even if you didn't want to come, you couldn't keep that boy of yours away."

Thinking about it after Adele had gone, Jenny knew it was true. And what about her? What about Jenny Carver? Would she really come back here again, or was this part of her life drawing to a close just as the month of July was?

On the evening before they were to leave, Jenny left Chris busily sorting through the treasures he planned to take home with him—blue-jay feathers, smooth stones, curiously gnarled pieces of roots—and walked out along the drive toward the fork in the road. She hesitated briefly, then began heading slowly in the direction of Ben's house. She hadn't seen him since the morning he'd carried her home. His silence had been a statement, louder than any spoken words, that he wasn't interested in her. But Jenny knew she couldn't bear to leave without seeing him one last time. Except with every step she began to feel less and less sure of herself and of the wisdom of what she was doing.

When she came close to the house the two dogs dashed out barking, but then, recognizing her, subsided into friendly sniffing and tail wagging. Even the tough, wary Blaze now treated her with guarded friendship. Chris would miss Blaze, she thought sadly. For a moment she hesitated, and then, before she lost courage completely, climbed the front steps and knocked on the door.

It took Ben a moment to answer, and when he did, she could tell she had interrupted him at some job around the house. He had a screwdriver in one hand and he was in jeans and a rumpled denim shirt. He was clearly surprised to see her, but then he arranged his expression into one of studied neutrality, as if he was deliberately suppressing all emotion.

"Well, hi there," he said.

"Hi." Jenny lingered in the doorway, and after a second's pause he opened it wider so she could come inside.

They stood in the hallway, hesitating, and at last Ben said, "I was just replacing a doorknob. Back door."

"Oh. I don't want to interrupt—"

"No, it's all right." He tossed the screwdriver onto the hall table and led the way into the living room.

"I wasn't going to stay, anyway," Jenny said tentatively, not sitting down. Her glance took in the mussed black hair, which he now ran his hand through, the beautiful eyes she had come to know so well and the strong chin with the faint cleft. Her heart thundered in her chest. His whole bearing was politely casual, noncommittal. "We're leaving tomorrow. I just wanted to say goodbye."

"I see." She heard the control, the careful indifference.

She hurried on, "And I wanted to thank you for being so kind to Chris. He's going back a different boy because of it."

"He's a great kid. I like him."

"It was still good of you to spend so much time with him."

He said simply, "When I was Chris's age somebody helped me. I know how much it means."

She suddenly felt a little bolder. "And you helped me, too. You made me look at myself. I'm afraid I saw things I didn't like very much."

She saw a muscle jump in his cheek. "I told you once you were too hard on yourself." He seemed to want to change the subject. "Tomorrow isn't the first of August, is it? Aren't you leaving a day early?"

"Yes, but my father and his wife will be coming on the first. I'd just as soon not be here for that."

He gave her a thoughtful look. "Sounds as if you still have a few things to work out."

She flushed under his steady direct gaze. "Perhaps. Someday." She stuck out her hand. "Well, goodbye, then."

"Goodbye, Jenny." He took her hand and held it for a moment, wrapping it in his own larger, stronger one. Then she pulled away and headed for the door.

"Jenny..."

She stopped, not turning. The room was silent.

"Aren't you going to kiss me goodbye?" he said after a moment.

He came up behind her and spun her around. Their glances locked, and she was surprised at the pain and longing she saw in his. She wanted to say something, to explain away the issues that had separated them, to make things right again between them, but her throat closed, the words refusing to come. He pulled her to him, his hands on her shoulders, then wrapped his arms around her as she tipped her face up to his. He brought his mouth down hard on hers, and the fingers of one hand buried themselves in the hair at the back of her head. Her own arms went around to press against his back, to bring him so close to her that nothing lay between them. Her mouth opened to his kiss, her whole being melting into his.

Then abruptly, he released her.

"Goodbye, Jenny," he said, and instead of seeing her to the door, he turned and strode toward the back of the house. For a moment she stood still, her mouth tingling with the memory of his. Then she slipped quietly out and walked into the twilight. The two dogs trotted at her heels until they came to the fork, then they, too, left her.

CHAPTER TEN

BACK IN BOSTON, summer slid into fall. The leaves turned scarlet and gold, then dropped to make way for November's leaden gray before Jenny paused to notice the passing of the seasons. Somehow there seemed less significance to such things in the city. Work, classes and studying left little room for opening her senses to beauty and change. And this year, there was the added feeling that everything important to her life had been left behind in Maine.

The day she'd returned she'd told Philip as kindly as possible that she was sorry, but she could never marry him. And now a hundred times a day she thought of Ben and pictured his reaction to some incident. She could even imagine him responding to a particularly dogmatic statement by a professor. *Doesn't conform to Sullivan's Law,* he would say with a smile in his voice. At night, when she was alone and tired, she often lay sleepless, remembering his touch, his kiss, his arms around her. She drove herself with determination, concentrating on the narrow path that her routine allowed her, letting the days slide by her, seldom bothering to stop and look around. The first break in the sameness came in mid-November when the phone rang.

"Jenny?"

"Yes. Who's this?"

"It's Grace Carmichael."

Jenny froze as she pictured the stepmother she'd never met but whom she'd imagined. A woman of considerable accomplishment, she was a doctor and years younger than Buzz Carmichael. Strong and directed, Jenny guessed, the very antithesis of her own mother with her sweetness, her even temper. Jenny swallowed and replied evenly, "Hello, Grace. How are you?"

"Fine and busy, which I'm sure applies to you, too. We were sorry to have missed you in Maine this summer."

Jenny, who was quite sure her father was anything but sorry, said levelly, "Yes, but we had to get back to Boston."

There was a brief pause at the other end. "I was wondering if you found the album, by any chance."

"The album?" Then Jenny remembered the carefully assembled collection of photographs she'd found in the guest cottage. All the lovingly arranged pictures of her and her parents had brought tears to her eyes. "I did come across it, yes," she said slowly.

"Oh, I'm so glad. But you should have taken it back with you. I made it for you."

Jenny was stunned. "You made it?"

"Yes, but that's all right. I've brought it back to Boston with me. I want you to have it."

"That's...that's very kind of you, Grace," Jenny stammered. The voice on the telephone was warm and friendly, not at all what she'd imagined.

"Only that's not really why I called." Again there was a slight hesitation. "Buzz and I are going to have Thanksgiving at home this year. And I was wondering if you and Chris would spend it with us. If you haven't already made plans, that is."

Jenny was completely dumbfounded. "I... No, we haven't made any plans." Despite herself, she found she couldn't help liking the owner of the voice on the other end of the line.

"Oh, please do come then. It would mean so much to your dad."

Jenny couldn't imagine that it would mean anything to him. How could he care about seeing someone he must remember only as an antagonistic teenager full of rage and rebellion? They had parted with such animosity—although, in fairness, she had to admit much of that had been hers.

Grace's voice was hurrying on. "And if there's someone else you'd care to bring along—a special friend, I mean—we'd be very happy to have him."

"Thank you," Jenny murmured, suddenly overcome by a familar pain around her heart. "But there's no one like that."

"You and Chris, then? You will come?"

"Yes, all right." Jenny drew a deep breath. "We'll come." She felt as if she had taken a plunge into deep water without knowing how to swim.

When she told Chris his reaction was gratifying.

"Hey, no kidding? My real grandfather?"

"That's right. And his wife. Her name is Grace."

"He's the one who owns the house in Maine," Chris said, thinking about it.

"Yes."

"Maybe he knows something about fly-fishing."

"Oh, he does."

"Hey, that's neat."

She was glad to see his enthusiasm. She was less optimistic, more apprehensive, but perhaps, she told herself, it was all part of a larger pessimism that had settled over her since their return to Boston. Somehow the life plan she'd set for herself—finishing her studies, becoming a full-fledged lawyer—mattered less to her now that the end was in sight. She had always, in good times and bad, been able to keep her eye focused on the next thing to be accomplished. Now she found that focus badly clouded, and she knew the reason. Images kept swimming into her line of vision—of dark blue eyes, black hair, a mobile mouth that could grin winningly or set itself with tantalizing firmness. Sometimes in the street she would see the tall lithe frame of a man striding along, and the set of his shoulders, the tilt of his head would make her heart pound until he turned to reveal a stranger's face. Then for days she would find it hard to concentrate, and a dark hopelessness would settle on her like a too-heavy coat on her shoulders, weighing her down.

Chris was the one cheerful element in her life now. Since returning from Maine he'd been happier and busier than she'd ever seen him. He had decided on his own to take a course in woodworking at school and had joined the school's hiking club. Often he was busy on weekends and would come home red-cheeked and exhilarated after an outing in which, Jenny guessed, he had been able to hold his own and perhaps show off some of his newly acquired skills.

As Thanksgiving approached, she grew anxious and apprehensive. What would she say to Grace? How would she make conversation with her father? And what on earth would she wear? She rooted through her closet, reminding herself that her finances would, under no circumstances, allow for anything new, although she made sure Chris had new pants and a sweater. Finally she decided on off-white wool slacks with a matching sweater. Then, because she felt a little color was needed, she found a silk scarf with tones of burgundy and green, and in a far corner of the same drawer a braided silk belt of burgundy. Turning in front of the mirror, she decided that the outfit would do.

In the end, it was easier than she could have imagined, largely due to the friendly presence of Grace, who met her warmly at the door and managed to make Buzz Carmichael give Jenny a hug and Chris a handshake. After that, thanks to Grace's sunny intervention, the day went more and more smoothly. She was a trim woman in her forties, bright-eyed and outgoing and full of laughter. Jenny took to her at once.

Chris did his share to break the ice by starting a discussion of fly-fishing with his dignified grandfather.

"You know, Grandpa, up there in Maine I used a gray ghost and a muddler minnow, but I had my best luck with a popper, believe it or not."

Buzz Carmichael, the terror of Boston courtrooms, stared with astonishment at his grandson and said gravely, "A popper. Now that's the little cork thing—bullet-shaped."

"Yup. And the bass seem to go for that quicker than anything."

Her father's face—older now but still handsome, Jenny thought with a pang of unexpected tenderness—grew softer as he regarded Chris. His gray cashmere pullover matched his silvery, brushed-back hair. His charcoal trousers were slim and well-tailored.

"I've had very good luck with poppers myself," he admitted.

The house was not one in which Jenny had grown up. It was slightly more contemporary in feeling but full of deep couches and chairs, striking abstract paintings and all kinds of books. A fire burned cheerfully in the hearth in the living room, and when they went into the dining room there was another fireplace, this one also alight with burning logs. Outside a thin snow was falling. The small group seated around the table had a tight-knit family look; an outsider would never have guessed how many emotional wounds were being healed.

"I can't take credit for the meal," Grace announced over the turkey. "Mrs. Detwiler, our housekeeper, got most of it ready yesterday and made lists of reminders for me so I'd put things in the oven at the right time. But I wanted her to have her own Thanksgiving."

"What kind of doctor are you?" Chris asked.

"A pediatrician."

"That means kids, right?"

"Right."

"Still like the dark meat, Jenny?" asked her father as he carved, and for the first time they exchanged a direct look.

"I do, but I've gotten to like almost anything." Jenny smiled. "Experience teaches, doesn't it?"

"It does, though sometimes a bit too slowly," he answered, looking down at the plate he was filling.

Grace bridged the moment with a question. "Do I understand you're almost finished with your studies, Jenny? January, isn't it?"

"Yes. Doing it part-time really stretched the whole business out, but I'm getting there at last."

"It'll mean all the more to you," Grace said. "That's the way I got to be a doctor."

"Really?" Jenny was surprised. Grace had such a stylish, competent look, which seemed to suggest she had traveled an easier road.

"Are you planning to stay with your present firm once you're qualified?" Buzz asked.

Jenny, still not over the novelty of her father's showing an interest in her, took the plate he handed her. "No. I'd thought I would, but circumstances have caused me to change my mind. Personal things. It seemed to me it would be a bit awkward..." She hesitated and saw a brief look dart between her father and Grace.

Then Buzz said gently but with characteristic forthrightness, "Ah. That Boyd fellow."

Jenny was startled. "Well, yes. Philip and I... How did you know that?"

He went on slicing, keeping his attention on the turkey. "Oh, well, you know. In our circle things get around."

So he *had* kept track of her, Jenny thought. He *had* cared what happened to her.

"It wasn't anything dreadful between us," she said. "I just didn't feel we were right for each other. And he's firmly entrenched there, so I'd really prefer to go with another firm."

Grace's hand came out to cover hers. "How wise of you."

Jenny felt moved and went on quickly, "Actually, I think Philip may go into politics. I hear he's been asked to run for the legislature. He'll like that."

Dishes were passed, plates heaped high. Outside, the thin icy snow began falling harder, snapping against the windows.

"Hey, this is neat!" Chris said with a smile, and Jenny saw her father smile back at him.

In the big modern kitchen, as they were clearing away dishes and taking a brief respite to make room for dessert, she said to Grace, "I want to thank you for making the album for me."

"Don't forget to take it with you when you go. I loved doing it."

"And for having us here." Jenny sorted silverware and started to fill the dishwasher. "You don't know how much it means to Chris."

"I can tell what it means to his grandfather. Listen to them, will you?"

They could hear the voices distantly.

"I'm taking this shop course—woodworking, you know?" Chris was saying. "But I can already do a lot of the stuff they're teaching."

"You're not by any chance the one who repaired the kitchen shelf up in the Maine house, are you?"

"Yup, I am. My friend Ben Sullivan showed me how to do things like that this summer."

"Oh, you know Ben?"

"Yes. Do you?"

Jenny, feeling herself blush, said to Grace, "We never should have waited this long, should we?"

Grace slid a quick look at her, then said, "No, of course not. But we were dealing with two pretty stubborn characters."

"I've done so many foolish things," Jenny said sadly.

"When you were young, yes, of course. Who hasn't?"

"But mine were serious. Running off and getting married at seventeen."

"Still, there's Chris to show for it, isn't there?" Grace began slicing a pumpkin pie. "I knew what Buzz was missing, not knowing his only grandchild. And being apart from you."

Jenny studied her stepmother. "You seem so right for Dad."

"My own thoughts exactly." Grace laughed. "As soon as I met him I knew he was the one. I was determined not to let him get away. We don't have that many chances for happiness in life, do we?" She swung around abruptly and reached for the whipped cream.

The snow had tapered off by the time they left, and the sky had cleared, leaving a pale moon and crisp night air. At the door her father gave Jenny a hug and said, "Now look, let's have lunch one day. We'll talk over this job business."

"And don't forget Christmas," Grace reminded her.

"All right," Jenny promised. "Yes to both."

Chris was quiet on the way home, and Jenny concentrated on driving over the slick streets. When they'd parked in the lot of their own apartment building, she turned to him and asked, "Well? Did you have a good time?"

He looked at her, and she could see the radiance in his face. "Yeah, it was great, wasn't it? I'm going to tell the guys in school about my grandfather. I mean, just that I had Thanksgiving with him. I won't brag or anything about him being famous and stuff."

She smiled back at him. "Maybe you're entitled to brag just a little bit," she said.

When she got into bed later it occurred to her that her life was like a jigsaw puzzle with all the jumbled pieces falling into place. When she had said goodbye to Philip, that had been one part of the picture straightening itself out. When she'd reconciled with her father and Grace that was another part. Finishing her studies and getting her law degree was still another. But right in the middle of the picture of Jenny Carver's life was the one jagged gap that refused to close. The missing heart of it. The one thing that would give meaning to all the rest.

He had never called, she thought as she lay there in the dark. All these months and he'd never called once.

We don't have that many chances for happiness in life, do we? Jenny could hear Grace's words as she curled in a tight ball in her cold bed and began to cry.

THE DAY SHE MET her father for lunch was a chilly one in early December, with snow spitting fitfully. Inside the elegant restaurant, however, all was warmth and comfort, muted voices and occasional laughter. Buzz was waiting for her at a table that she suspected was always reserved for him—set with spotless white linen, sparkling silver and glassware. Jenny felt touched when he stood up and kissed her cheek lightly, and she couldn't stop the small nudge of pride she felt when heads turned their way. He was in a dark gray suit with a tiny stripe of red woven in. Immaculate white cuffs showed at his wrists.

They sat by a window with a view of the winter-bound city, eating thin slices of grilled chicken breast on a bed of greens and asparagus along with rice pilaf. Hot coffee arrived in a heavy silver pot, and both of them said no to dessert.

"You're so thin," he said critically. "No reason for you to refuse dessert. Grace would have my hide if I had dessert, though."

"She's keeping you very fit." Jenny smiled. "Have I mentioned how lucky you are to have her?"

"No need to mention it—I know it."

"Works both ways," she said, and reached out to pat his hand, still feeling the wonder of their being friends again.

"Well, then, let's both order crème brûlée and worry about the consequences later," he said, signaling the waiter back.

"I'd better warn you," he said moments later as they dipped into the rich confection, "Chris and I have something planned for early spring. A fishing trip."

"Really? I'm so glad. He seems like a different boy since we got back from Maine."

"I suspect he's not the only one who's different."

Jenny put down her spoon and gave him a questioning look.

"Is it that obvious?"

"No, just a guess," he said airily. "After all, I don't know you that well anymore."

"I had a hard time even talking Chris into coming back."

"What about you?"

"You *are* persistent, you know that?" She grinned. "Well, the answer is no. I didn't go through all those years of law school to give up now."

"Wouldn't expect you to. And if what you really want is to stay in Boston, I'm sure there'll be a place for you. Not that I want to advise you—you're doing fine on your own. But I never should have shut you out all those years ago. That was my fault. And I'd like to help now to make up for it." Abruptly he changed the subject. "What about Ben Sullivan?"

Jenny reddened and looked down at the heavy tablecloth. "Dad, I really don't think I can—"

"No—forget I said it," he said with a wave of one long-fingered hand. "None of my business. But Grace thought—you know, woman's intuition or some such—that maybe there was something between you and Ben."

In spite of her confusion, Jenny was curious. "You know him well, don't you?"

"Yes. His whole family, too. First-class lawyer. Always thought a lot of Ben." The deep-set eyes studied her for a moment. "Look, forget I mentioned it. None of my business, as I said."

"No, it's all right," Jenny insisted. "It's just that, uh, nothing's been said—between us. Before I met him, I thought everything I wanted was right here in Boston and would come once I had my law degree...." Her voice trailed off.

"And now you're not so sure?"

She shook her head slowly, not trusting her voice for a moment and finally saying, "No, I'm not."

"Good," he said. "Doesn't do to have too many ideas set in concrete. Look where it got me. Nearly cost me the two people who mattered most to me."

She gazed across the table at him, her eyes misty. "I'm glad we're back together, Dad."

Buzz Carmichael cleared his throat loudly. "Well, whatever you decide, I know it'll be the right thing."

Jenny wished she could be as sure. But talking of Ben, even in such an oblique way, disturbed her and brought back memories that carried a painful sweetness with them. Standing on his front porch with her coffee cup in her hand while he studied her seriously. The strong fluid motion of his arm as he showed Chris how to make a cast. His presence behind her in the canoe that night as he propelled them silently across the black-and-silver water.

But he'd never called, had he? She reminded herself of that as she came reluctantly back to earth. And the light-years' distance between Boston and Tucker's Pond was the same stumbling block it had always been.

A week later Chris went on a hiking weekend with his club. They were to take a bus out of the city and then hike to a horse farm ten miles away where they would be put up for the night, returning late Sunday. Each boy was to bring a sleeping bag. Excitement ran high, and Chris planned to spend Friday night with a friend so they could be together and awake early for the bus. Jenny experienced no more than normal apprehension. After the evidence of maturity she'd seen in her son, she had few worries these days about him. And a three-day weekend to herself would be ideal for studying.

On Friday evening, she spread books and papers out on the desk in her bedroom and immersed herself in them as soon as Chris had left. Somewhere along the way she grew drowsy and dozed off. The telephone shrilling in her ear caused her to sit up in confusion.

"Hello?"

"Jenny Carver?" A man's voice, deep but tentative, as if he wasn't sure he was calling the right place. Jenny, still only half-awake, felt her heart leap into her throat.

"This is Jenny Carver."

"Ah, good. This is Roger Trask. We haven't met, but I'm with the firm of Henkle, Bloodworth, Starnes and Trask."

Disappointment crashed through Jenny. Until that moment she hadn't realized how desperately she'd been longing to hear one particular male voice. She kept a tight grip on the telephone. "Yes, Mr. Trask?"

"I understand you're planning to change your affiliation once you have your law degree next month. Actually, I guess I should admit I had lunch with your dad the other day, and the subject came up."

"I see."

"I was hoping you might come around to talk with us before you make any new commitment. I realize this is long-range planning, but we'd be pleased to have you come and meet with us here informally..."

His voice went on pleasantly. No promises on either side, but they really would enjoy...and another Carmichael entering the law was good news...of course her dad probably had the right of a first refusal, but just in case...

Jenny thanked him for the suggestion and promised to call after the holidays. Then she put down the receiver and stood up. Hugging herself, she crossed to the window and looked out over the wintry city streets, listening to the wind as it whipped between the buildings.

A few months ago even to be considered for a position with such a law firm would have put her on cloud nine. Now the call was only a disappointment, something that had made her heart drop, because the voice on the telephone had been the wrong voice.

Instead of returning to her desk, she went over to her bed and dropped onto it, her arms still crossed in front of her. For a long time she lay there, feeling colder and colder in spite of the warmth of the room.

We don't have that many chances for happiness in life, do we?

She drifted off and awoke with a start sometime later, the taste of disappointment still on her tongue. The room was dark except for her desk lamp. She got up and went to the telephone, picked it up hesitantly and then put it down again. For a few seconds she stood there, thinking. Then she went to the closet, took out a pair of warm slacks and began to change, moving quickly and decisively.

Twenty-five miles north on the interstate she began to tell herself she was every kind of a fool, starting out like this in the middle of the night, but she made no move to slow down or turn back. If she was a fool, there was no help for it now. Anything was better than not knowing. She should have called, of course. Any sensible person would have. But it wouldn't have been good enough to just hear his voice. She had to see him, to touch him, to find out whether things between them had been real or if it had evaporated with the summer.

As she entered New Hampshire it began to snow. Jenny put on the windshield wipers and turned up the defroster. On the radio she heard a weather report. Scattered snow throughout New England, a voice told her, heavier toward the north. Jenny leaned forward and drove carefully through the night.

The sky was lightening by the time she reached Tucker's Pond. Snow was still falling, but more thinly now. She heard a snowplow somewhere in the distance, but along the main street her tracks were the first ones. The snow was not deep enough to make the roads impassable, but Jenny was cramped from holding tightly to the wheel and peering ahead. She drove through town to the county highway, then turned off onto the dirt road that had become so familiar to her. Here her snow tires were able to bite through to the rough surface underneath, and she skidded only slightly once or twice. She passed the fork in the road and saw her father's house, white-blanketed and alien-looking in its winter setting. She gave it only a glance and inched along the narrow road until she pulled up in front of Ben's house. Weary and suddenly full of misgivings, she let her head drop forward on her hands as they gripped the wheel. Maybe coming here was a terrible mistake. Maybe he'd been only too glad to see the last of her. Wouldn't he have called if she'd really meant something to him?

She sat back and took a deep breath. Then she climbed out of the car and made her way up the snowy path to the front porch and knocked on the door. Instantly the dogs began to bark. It seemed like an eternity before the door opened.

Ben stood there wearing a heavy gray sweater and dark blue corduroy pants. His hair was mussed. Rocket and Blaze were at his side, tails wagging. For a moment he stared at Jenny without speaking as she anxiously tried to read his expression. Finally, letting his eyes travel over her, he said, "You didn't bring your coffee cup."

She shook her head slowly, never taking her eyes from his face. "Oh, Ben..."

"I've just put the pot on in the kitchen," he said. "Come in."

She took a tentative step inside and he closed the door behind her. Gazes locked, the two of them stood in the little hall with the dogs crowding them.

"Jenny," he said at last. Only her name, and then he drew her into his arms. His kiss was soft and cautious at first, then turned strong and passionate as Jenny responded with an abandon she had not known was in her.

"Jenny, Jenny." He held her tight, bent his head to bury his face in her neck, kissed her again. Then he grabbed at the zipper of her down jacket, pulled it down and yanked the jacket off, pressing her to him again and letting his hands slide up and down her back and through her hair. He murmured, "I don't care why you came or how long you're staying or what it all means, but you're here and I love you."

"Oh, Ben, I love you, too. That's why I came. Because it wasn't good enough to telephone. I had to see you. I just had to—" His lips covered hers again, parting them insistently and tasting her mouth as if he had been thirsting for it.

Some time later he said, "You must have driven all night."

"Most of it. I couldn't sleep. I couldn't live through another day without you."

"You don't know how many times I've wanted to call you."

"Oh, Ben, why didn't you?"

"I suppose because I'm some kind of an idiot."

She put both hands up to hold his face so she could look at it. She felt as if she was memorizing something important.

"Could that coffee wait?" she whispered.

The bed was still unmade and the imprint of his head was on the pillow as Jenny lowered herself onto the mattress. She turned to breathe in the scent of him and press her lips to it. He gave a low laugh as he lowered himself beside her and said, "Hey, we can do better than that." He surveyed her heavy sweater and wool slacks. "Boy, you're really bundled up, aren't you?"

"I missed that laugh," she whispered, holding up her arms and letting him pull the sweater over her head. "When I first met you, you were so serious, and then later all I could remember was your laugh." They helped each other, shedding clothes and drawing in close under the covers.

"I woke up so many nights and tried to imagine your head on the pillow next to mine," Jenny said.

"Is the reality as good?"

She raised herself on one elbow and kissed him, then pulled his head against her breasts. Four long months, she thought. And she'd known it way back then. Why couldn't she have admitted it to herself? Then she shut out all thinking and gave herself over to pure feeling, listening only to her own heartbeat and his voice repeating her name softly, against her skin.

LATER SHE SLEPT, but briefly, waking in his arms and lifting her face to find his lips again.

"You must be worn out," he murmured. "You didn't sleep last night." His hands moved over her body, tracing the line of her breasts and hips as she lay on her side facing him.

"I'm not. I feel wonderful." She ran a hand through his hair. "What were you going to do today before I got here?"

"Nothing this good. And nothing important. I haven't done anything important since you left. None of it meant anything without you."

She let her gaze travel around the room. She'd never seen his bedroom before. Comfortable, like the rest of the house. Book-strewn but still tidy. A desk in one corner.

"What was the real reason you didn't call me?" she asked.

He waited a moment before answering. His hand was on her shoulder, kneading it gently, almost as if he had to touch her to reassure himself of her presence.

"Guilt, I guess."

"Guilt! But why? I was the one who—"

"You didn't do anything. Anything wrong, that is. I was the one who came charging in, making demands, wanting you to change your whole life overnight."

"You never made demands."

"Maybe only implied. But it still wasn't fair. I put too much pressure on you. That day you told me off, you reminded me you'd been making hard decisions all your life. And I realized it was true. You had your life all planned one way and you'd worked damned hard for it. What right did I have to crash in and break everything up? Even that guy Philip. . ."

"Philip's history," she murmured. "I told him so the day I got back to Boston."

"Oh, Jenny—that long ago?" He bent to kiss her again, smoothing her hair back gently.

"None of my life meant anything without you."

"When time began to go by, I thought you'd fallen back into your work and that you and Philip were making your plans. It just seemed too late. But I saw your head on that pillow plenty of times, too. And you know something? It's the first time I've ever been lonely in this house."

Jenny lifted her face to him again, begging another kiss.

"You'd better sleep some more," he whispered.

"Not just yet," she murmured, rolling over on top of him and letting her hair fall around his face.

She drifted in and out of sleep, but he was always there when she awoke.

"Where's Chris?" he asked once.

"Gone on a hike. He's a world-class hiker now. I left a note for him in case he gets back ahead of me. Told him if he needs anything to call his grandfather."

"His grandfather. . . You're kidding."

"No. That's another little matter I really messed up."

"Jenny. Don't I always tell you you're too hard on yourself? It takes two for that kind of misunderstanding. Tell me what happened."

She related the story, from Grace's Thanksgiving invitation through to lunch with her father.

"And now you're friends again?"

"Yes. And I love Grace. It's like having a sister."

He said, "When they were here in August, Buzz and I did a little fishing together. We usually talk about flies and the law and stay pretty far away from personal things. Even so, I got the feeling he wasn't as inflexible as he used to be. I think Grace has been good for him."

She was quiet for a moment, wrapped close in his arms. "That night in the cabin, the night you found me and carried me there... I thought you were so angry with me. I thought you never wanted to see me again."

"Oh, God. I was half-crazy with worry when I found you like that. I was so afraid you were badly hurt. But I didn't want to use the situation as an excuse to pressure you even more. You didn't owe me anything."

"I can't believe the time we've wasted."

He grinned at her. "Well, we're not wasting any time now."

Presently he got up, pulled on his clothes and went downstairs for coffee, bringing back two mugs. The dogs trailed cautiously at his heels, poking their heads in to look at her briefly before settling down in the hall outside the door.

"I made fresh," he said, sitting on the edge of the bed.

Jenny sat up and took the mug he held out.

"This is only to tide us over," he explained. "I'm going to make us a real breakfast." His face grew serious and he went on, "Darling, the one thing I don't want is for you to feel you're being pulled in two directions at once."

The *darling* rang in her ears. "I won't, I promise. Don't worry about it."

"No, I want to say this. I'm perfectly willing to come back to Boston to live. Your work is there, and I know Boston well. It wouldn't be hard for me to readjust."

She looked at him with disbelief. "It would be impossible," she said flatly. "You don't belong there. You belong here. And I've come to believe I do, too. And Chris."

"It's a pretty big change. Not that there isn't plenty of work. As a matter of fact, I've advertised for an associate."

"You've what?"

"Well, I've taken on a case involving one of the big lumber companies in the northern part of the state. It'll mean travel and a lot of extra hours of work. Also, I promised to do a lecture series at the university, so that has to be worked in."

"Are you really interviewing people?"

"I've seen two—a couple of bright young law graduates."

She looked at him over the rim of the mug. "Call them up and tell them the job's taken."

He studied her seriously. "Have you really thought about this?"

"I've thought of nothing else for months."

His smile encompassed her, surrounded her, warmed her with its love.

"Besides," she said, "it'll make it easier to change your sign."

"My sign?"

"On your office door. Sullivan and Sullivan. Sounds good, doesn't it?"

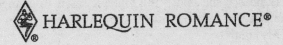

HARLEQUIN ROMANCE®

brings you

Stories that celebrate love, families and children!

Watch for our next Kids & Kisses title in November!

Who's Holding the Baby?
by Day Leclaire
Harlequin Romance #3338

Everybody loves this baby—but who's supposed to be looking after her? A delightful and very funny romance from the author of To Catch a Ghost *and* Once A Cowboy....

Toni's only three months old, and already she needs a scorecard to keep track of the people in her life! She's been temporarily left with her uncle Luc, who's recruited his secretary Grace, who's pretending to be his fiancée, hoping to mollify the police, who've called the child-welfare people, who believe that Grace and Luc are married! And then life starts to get *really* complicated....

Available wherever Harlequin books are sold.

 <!-- (KIDS & KISSES logo) -->

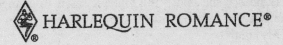 <!-- (Harlequin logo) -->

HARLEQUIN SUPERROMANCE®

WHERE ARE THEY NOW?

It's sixteen years since the CLASS OF '78 graduated
from Berkeley School for Girls. On that day, four young
women, four close friends, stood on the brink of
adulthood and dreamed about the directions their lives
might take. None could know what lay ahead....

Now it's time to catch up with Sandra, Laurel, Meg and Kim.
Each woman's story is told in Harlequin Superromance's
new miniseries, THE CLASS OF '78.

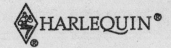

EDGE OF ETERNITY
Jasmine Cresswell

Two years after their divorce, David Powell and Eve Graham met again in Eternity, Massachusetts—and this time there was magic between them. But David was tied up in a murder that no amount of small-town gossip could free him from. When Eve was pulled into the frenzy, he knew he had to come up with some answers—including how to convince her they should marry again...this time for keeps.

EDGE OF ETERNITY, available in November from Intrigue, is the sixth book in Harlequin's exciting new cross-line series, **WEDDINGS, INC.**

Be sure to look for the final book, **VOWS,** by Margaret Moore (Harlequin Historical #248), coming in December.

HOLLYWOOD

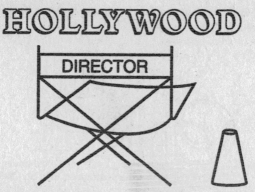

Coming this Fall—
Harlequin Movies on TV!

If you like a good romance you'll *love* the brand-new
Harlequin movies that will be airing on the CBS network on
Sunday afternoons this Fall!

These full-length *romantic* movies are based on Harlequin
novels written by some of your favorite authors! They're
entertaining romances with lots of twists and turns and
guaranteed to keep you riveted to your seat, so watch for
them!

As a Reader Service member you'll be hearing more about
these Harlequin movies in the months to come. Next month's
Heart to Heart newsletter, for example, will bring you more
specific details, along with information about the exciting
prizes you could win in the all new

"Harlequin Goes to Hollywood" Sweepstakes!

CBSBPA

This November, share the passion with *New York Times* Bestselling Author

Sandra Brown

(previously published under the pseudonym Erin St. Claire)

in

THE DEVIL'S OWN

Kerry Bishop was a good samaritan with a wild plan. Linc O'Neal was a photojournalist with a big heart.

Their scheme to save nine orphans from a hazardos land was foolhardy at best—deadly at the worst.

But together they would battle the odds—and the burning hungers—that made the steamy days and sultry nights doubly dangerous.

Reach for the brightest star in women's fiction with

MIRA ™

MSBDO-R